GODFORSAKEN

Leo Anthony

authorHOUSE®

AuthorHouse™
1663 Liberty Drive
Bloomington, IN 47403
www.authorhouse.com
Phone: 1-800-839-8640

First published by AuthorHouse 10/5/2010

ISBN: 978-1-4520-7326-2 (sc)
ISBN: 978-1-4520-7563-1 (e)

Library of Congress Control Number: 2010912443

Printed in the United States of America

This book is printed on acid-free paper.

Because of the dynamic nature of the Internet, any Web addresses or
links contained in this book may have changed since publication and
may no longer be valid. The views expressed in this work are solely those
of the author and do not necessarily reflect the views of the publisher,
and the publisher hereby disclaims any responsibility for them.

This book is dedicated to my Mom, because there's no greater love than the love of a mother.

When You Cry
Who Do You Cry To?

CONTENTS

Preface   ix
Chapter 1   1
Chapter 2   5
Chapter 3   11
Chapter 4   17
Chapter 5   21
Chapter 6   29
Chapter 7   34
Chapter 8   43
Chapter 9   49
Chapter 10   56
Chapter 11   67
Chapter 12   77
Chapter 13   83
Chapter 14   91
Chapter 15   107
Chapter 16   119
Chapter 17   128
Chapter 18   134
Chapter 19   147
Chapter 20   161
Chapter 21   171
Chapter 22   186

PREFACE

As I walk along the shore, I can feel the water passing over my feet as the waves roll in. Each time the cold water touches me, it chills my body as if it were freezing my bones. I can feel the wet sand between my toes and the seashells under my feet. In the shallowest of waters, I'm in my deepest of thoughts. The sky is filled with a mixture of red, orange, and purple lights, as if it were painted. Behind me is a couple sitting on the beach enjoying the sunset. I can see how mortals would find this romantic, but after millions of sunsets, you lose the attraction. Although their heads are filled with a cluster of emotions, you can see the love in their eyes.

Is it so simple for them to love, for them to give

their hearts and open their minds to someone else? Is everything based on love—our mindset, our development, and our actions? It seems throughout the history of mankind every war, book, poem, painting, and even song started on that little feeling. How can we lose control over our actions based on this emotion? I haven't always questioned love; I was the sole creator of it. My heart was open to love everything and anything; but tragically, he decided to take advantage of it. My name is Sophia, and it all started with him—Lucifer.

CHAPTER 1

When the Earth was but a baby, I roamed this planet all alone, learning its sophistication. I never could have imagined the potential this piece of rock had when I created it. All I did was plant the seed and this beautiful planet grew. The land sprouted with all types of plant life. There were trees so tall that when you climbed to the top, you'd be sitting in a cloud. There were many different types of flowers; each resembled a perfume bottle with a unique shape, color, and smell. The large holes were filled with water—water so crystal clear you see the bottom no matter how deep. Last but not least was a breeze, a breeze so tender it would soothe your soul.

I spent many years exploring all the beauties. I

would lie on the shores, dry up in the sun, and fall asleep with the motion of the breeze. But there was something missing; there was so much to offer, and none of it was being used. The land, ocean, and sky were empty. I couldn't help but feel that something so beautiful needed to be enjoyed. I then decided to produce living, breathing creatures, which would utilize all the natural splendors this planet reared.

I went and handpicked the most vibrant and evasive flowers I could find. I held each flower in my palm one by one, breathing life into the flower. A light would shine, and when the light went away, I would be holding a newborn creature. Each time I did this, I would think of a new creature to create. Each animal came out just as beautiful as each flower I used.

When I was finished, the water was filled with hundreds of different animals. There were sea creatures that had fins, gills, and even long tails. Some were little and swam through the waters like torpedoes, while others were large, gentle, and moved with the energy of a snail. So I spent time with each one, learning what they had to offer. Soon I was zipping through the seas, racing in and out of the current. The sun would shine down, illuminating the coral with neon lights, giving it the most electrifying glow. When I was finished with my underwater explorations, I would lie on the backs of my gentle sea giants and look up at the evening sky. Every time they took a deep breath of air I could feel their hearts beat. It was like lying down on a big rocking chair.

Not only stars could soar across the sky—now there were all types of winged animals. Some were as big as an elephant, and others were as small as a flea, and many had feathers displaying all types of different patterns. While observing them, I learned how to fly. You must be wondering one of two things: humans can't fly, and if I could fly, why was I just learning about it then? The answers are simple: I'm not human, and I never had a reason. This is where the art of dance was originated; imagine dancing on the clouds in the most beautiful dress you could find. This was what flying felt like.

Land animals were truly amazing; they had a very different structure with so many variations. Some were large, furry, scaly, and colorful; but they possessed something the others lacked—the heart of a warrior. These animals weren't afraid to leave their realm and jump in the water or climb up the tallest tree. They each explored the ends of the Earth looking for homes in all the places ascertainable. From them I learned how to develop my body into top physical performance. I was able to climb up trees with one jump, run across the plains without being noticed, and leap down cliffs, always landing on my feet. Despite all my physical growth, I was always expanding my mental growth as well.

The one observation that always dwelled on my mind was that no matter what type of creature, after procreating, each species would stay and form herds together. As time passed, each herd's numbers grew, and more and more of these animals were living amongst each other in harmony. Every night as I watched each animal scurry back to its respective family, I would lay back and stare at the stars. At this time I didn't know it, but the feeling I had was loneliness. I had no one to share my eternity with—no one to learn from, teach, or even speak with. As I stared at the North Star with my head resting on a flat rock, I could feel the grass underneath my body. Every time I twisted and turned, they tickled me like tiny masseurs. I jumped up; it finally came to me. I needed a herd, someone to enjoy this eternity; someone to enjoy me.

CHAPTER 2

Now I didn't know where to begin, much less how to begin. But I did know what I wanted the outcome to be.

I traveled across this planet looking for a place in which I would be in solitude, for complete concentration would increase the probability in a successful outcome. I traveled through jungles, forest, deserts, and caves. I finally found it—a mountain. This mountain is current-day Mount Everest. I climbed to the top, so high that none of my previous creatures had traveled up there. When I reached the top, it was the highest point on the Earth. The ground was covered in fluorescent white snow, and the breeze was unbelievable. You could even see your breath; every time I took a deep breath, it looked like the exhaust pipe of a factory in an industrial city. It was so quiet you could almost hear the snowflakes as they dwindled through the air and hit the floor.

I sat there on a small pile of snow. For weeks I sat in the same spot, until the snow built up and around me; I was like a fly in an ice cube. I was alone with my thoughts. I devised a plan, in which I was going to not create an animal but to give a part of me in order to give life to another being—a being just like me, one who could have my strength and immortality.

First I realized one being wasn't enough. But I couldn't come up with an exact number. I realized when thinking back to the herds that there were tons of them. I wasn't sure how many to create, whether twenty beings or just two. After thinking about it for a while, I realized the perfect number would be five, for five is the number of points on the Earth. People currently know of four, but there are actually five points; there is the north point, the south point, the east point, the west point, and the center point. No one knows of the center point, but it's the most important point. It's where all of the other points connect. Now that I knew how many

I wanted to create, I needed to know how—and then it came to me.

I took a deep breath in and blew out with all the force my lungs contained. All the snow around and on top of me blew away. It finally hit me; I needed to use my fingers. Your fingers descend from your palm, and my palm is where my power to give life comes from. So by giving the flesh and blood straight from that area, I would be able to give them life as well as all my powers. I decided to give them all my powers except one; the power of life. I can turn a rock into a bird and make a dead wolf howl again; this is a power I feel that no one else should possess. It's too strong of a power, and I can't risk allowing someone to misuse it.

Being immortal means I heal immediately. I wouldn't normally even get cut; the only reason I would have any injury is because I am in inflicting the injury myself. Being so powerful can actually overpower my own immortality, but I will heal back. So I made a fist and punched through the frozen layer of ice on the ground and pulled out a sharp shard of frozen rock. I laid my left hand down on the ice and made one swift blow. All five fingers were severed right off; within moments my body regenerated new fingers. I picked up the five severed fingers and walked over to five piles of snow and dropped one finger in each pile.

You could see the snow around the fingers turning red. The blood was slowly seeping into the white snow around it, looking like the smoke of a campfire mixing with the air. Then the snow started to melt, and you could see the fingers again. Except this time they each had a knuckle. Suddenly each piece changed. Their sizes and color were changing; at the same time, they were growing. The knuckle sprouted a hand, which sprouted an arm. The arm grew into a torso, and then legs appeared. Last but not least their backs ripped open, and wings opened up. Within seconds there were five fully grown angels: Michael, Raphael, Gabriel, Uriel, and Lucifer. Just like each name, they were all different.

Michael is six feet and two inches tall and built like a statue. His body was very muscular. He has piercing blue eyes and bright blonde hair. His face always has this serious expression. He actually has a very nice smile, but it's very rare that you see it. His complexion is very pale, like the color of milk; you can even see pink tones on his cheeks, elbows, and knuckles.

Raphael is six feet tall. His build is close to

Michael's, well defined but not as muscular. He has green eyes and light brown hair. He is also very light, but not as light as Michael; and it isn't that rare to see a smile on his face.

Gabriel is six feet and one inch tall. His body is built, but he has a little stomach; he isn't fat but is not as toned as Raphael or Michael is. He has hazel eyes, dark brown hair, and is the same complexion as Raphael.

Uriel is six feet and three inches tall, with a very thin build. He is well defined but lacks mass. His eyes are gray, and his hair is red. He is the only one who has freckles, and his face comes with a permanent smile.

Lucifer is six feet and two inches tall and well built. His body is so defined you can even see the muscles in his fingers. His eyes are dark brown. Even though he has the darkest eyes, you can still see the fire burning in them. He has straight black hair. He also has dimples. Every time he smiles or speaks, they just pop out at you. Unlike the rest, he isn't that light. His skin is olive toned; this almost gives him a glow.

Looking at them made me realize how different I looked. I'm only five feet and two inches tall. I'm not muscular at all; in fact, I'm kind of curvy. I have blue eyes and straight brown hair. I am also light skinned. They were five completely different people—different from each other and different from me.

CHAPTER 3

During the following few centuries, we explored self-expression. Open up your soul and let it pour out like a waterfall, for self-expression is the true masterpiece of life. The first thing we did was create a language. The language is called Aleos; it's an ancient language, and we are currently the only ones who can speak it, although I may be a little rusty. Aleos wasn't just a language we spoke, but it also had a writing system.

Not too long after creating Aleos, we began composing our feelings into physical forms. These were the primitive forms of fine arts, such as music, dance, and painting. I loved painting; we used to paint pictures on the bark of trees and on surfaces of stones using a paste we made from flower petals, leaves, and berries. My pictures would always be a reflection of the way I felt, whether it would show in the color, blending, or even brush strokes.

As the years went by, we grew accustomed to each other's company. They were my best friends—actually, at that time my only friends. But for some reason I always felt a strange attraction to Lucifer. You see, then I didn't know it was an attraction, but he always appealed to me differently.

Lucifer was the complete opposite from the others and from me, but for some reason I liked that. I didn't understand him, which made nothing predictable, such as when I saw them all playing with the bees. Michael, Gabriel, Uriel, and Raphael would watch them but not disturb them. They would only look and take notes; they acquired by observation. But Lucifer was the complete opposite. When he saw the bee, he let it sting him. Lucifer didn't want to only observe it; he wanted to feel it. He learned by living; he wanted to feel everything, from pleasure to pain.

It was those kinds of actions that caught my attention. I admired this quality. I used to sit there for hours and watch him as he played with nature, but over time I started to develop feelings for him—feelings I had never had before. Slowly curiosity began to consume me, and I had to learn more about him. I didn't want to observe him but rather let him sting me; and this moment changed me forever.

The sun had gone down a few hours before, so the sky had a deep blue tone to it, but the stars were extra bright, making the sky look like a Christmas tree. I was walking by the beach, dragging my feet through the water. It was a little chilly; you could see the white air every time you breathed out. I had my arms folded looking into the sky, watching the birds flying across the waters. The only thing you could hear were the sounds of the alligators in the water about ten feet away from me. They were making a bellowing sound; oddly enough, it was quite soothing. Then there was a moment of silence followed by a loud splash. About seventy feet away, a giant sea monster jumped out the water and crashed back in. The creature was about forty feet long and able to scare all the alligators away. After the large splash, it surfaced, its long neck arched and its tail floating behind it looking like a snake. It was staring at the water for about twelve seconds before another splash, except this splash was very little, at least very little compared to this creature's, and up came Lucifer.

He was swimming with the giant sea monster. Nothing scared him. He loved every animal, no matter how big or aggressive. In a way, every animal sort of respected him. He saw me and began to swim my way; the creature made a grunt and swam the opposite direction. I looked at him as he got closer and closer.

When he reached me, he came out of the water, and his body was dripping wet. His chest was covered with goose bumps, and every breath he took sent a drop of water running down his chest. But the speed in which each drop traveled began to slow as it would have to pass over each abdomen muscle, one at a time. I never realized the true beauty of the human form, but looking at him, standing in front of me, breathing heavily, I couldn't help but to admire the natural work of art he was.

When our eyes met, I gave him a serious look. He then scooped his hand through his hair and splashed the water at me; and as the cold water hit me, my body jumped and I gave a little giggle.

"Why are you walking alone?" he asked.

"There's no better company than the company of your thoughts."

"Would you mind the company of my thoughts?"

"It's not your thoughts that I mind." I smiled and then turned around. I had no excuse for avoiding him this time and no place to go.

He laughed and then said, "Lucky for me, my only thoughts are of you." I didn't get what was going on, but I was sure whatever I was feeling, he was feeling as well.

"You are so peaceful with even the most aggressive of animals."

"Is it not you who taught us to care for every living creature?"

"But of course. I created every living creature, and I care for all my creations."

"Did you not create me?"

"No."

"No?"

"Everything I created, I control. You are not a rose, nor a snake. I don't control you."

"Sophia, you don't have to control everything."

"Control allows me to understand. I understand the way they act, why they act that way, and what they will do. You I do not understand."

"Let your feelings guide you. You don't have to know what to expect. Just know what you want."

As I turned around and began to take my first step away from him, I felt a shiver. The shiver ran up my arm, down my spine, and into my toes. I looked at my wrist, and his hand was on it. That second when he grabbed my wrist, all I felt was raw power surge through me. I didn't understand the sensation; it was a mixture of pain and pleasure. I never knew the extent of how powerful he was; from that moment, his presence became a part of me, and I will forever be able to sense when he is around.

How is it that I am the creator of life, and his touch just brought me to life? It was as if I was a puppet and he made me human. My brain was telling me to leave, and I pulled my arm away from him.

Then he said, "Don't go."

I turned and looked into his eyes; I then realized he wanted me, and I was his.

CHAPTER 4

That night we just laid there, looking up at the stars. Secured in his arms, I rested my head on his chest and fell asleep to the rhythm of his heartbeat.

The next morning when I woke up, Lucifer was still sleeping. I decided not to wake him; I went for a walk to sort out my thoughts. I loved him and felt he was a conquest I deserved to explore. We each love someone and should not be afraid of it, for love should not be hidden or denied; no matter who it is we love.

I decided that the others needed to know. I didn't want their relationship to change. The five of them were close friends, and I didn't want them to treat Lucifer any differently because of the extra attention he would be receiving.

When I arrived, they were all laying down in a small clearing surrounded by trees. I said, "We need to talk." They all sat up straight and looked at me. I began to explain. "Lately I've been very curious. I've been getting feelings, and I haven't yet to explore them."

"What kind of feelings?" Michael asked me.

"It's hard to explain. I barely understand them myself."

"Just speak as how you feel," Raphael said. His words were a way of reassurance.

"All right, well I love Lucifer." I didn't mean to just blurt out the statement, but it came out the same way it was going through my head.

"Love?"

"Well I can't quite articulate this feeling. It's a feeling you can't explain. You have to feel it before you can understand what I mean." I didn't want to complicate things, so I thought carefully on what to say next. "It's like ..." and in the middle of my sentence Lucifer walked in. When my eyes caught his, I didn't know how to finish my sentence. I just turned and said, "I think we should talk about this another day."

I didn't mean to just dismiss the conversation; I just didn't know how to explain to them the feelings

I was having, since they had never experienced it themselves. Love can be very tricky, but only a person in love will understand what love can make you do. I never got to finishing up this conversation, and I'm glad I didn't.

As Lucifer and I got closer, a rift was forming, and slowly the other angels would shun him. Aggression filled the air, and every day became a competition. I didn't understand why they got so competitive. It's not like I'm a trophy. My love can't be won from a race. But they didn't realize this at the time, nor did I realize that the competition was about more than just me.

Everything they did was like an Olympic event. It became so hostile that they took the beauty out of painting. When Lucifer would paint a picture, the others would try and paint better. It wasn't the paintings themselves that I loved about Lucifer's but why he did it. Actually, Michael's paintings would come out so lifelike it looked like a photograph. Lucifer would make each brushstroke distinct from the previous stroke. None of the colors would blend into the next, but after looking at the whole painting, you would be able to see what it was. Lucifer always told me, "You have to look at the whole picture before you can see its beauty." His outlook is what made me love the things he did.

Although I never commented nor compared their work, they were at constant war. I knew I had to do something to stop them from feuding, but I didn't want to. Lucifer and I were getting closer, and I didn't want it to change; but deep down inside I knew I needed to fix things between them for the better. It's funny how love can make you selfish, although your judgment isn't deliberately selfish; it's the feeling you don't want to lose. So after winning the debate with my heart, I decided that Lucifer and I needed to have a conversation and I would do what needed to be done.

Chapter 5

I sat the by the water throwing rocks into the river and listening to it splash. For some reason, the sound of water was so soothing. When Lucifer walked over, he noticed what I was doing.

"Sophia, did you ever notice that you find the strangest sounds soothing?"

"I'm surprised you noticed," I said as I laughed.

"It's hard not to notice nature's most beautiful work of art," said Lucifer. How does one feel stressed when one has someone like him around? Everything he said just fit together so perfectly. Each word made me feel more and more at ease.

"I don't know, it's something about listening to water that puts my soul at ease." It's true; I've always loved the sound of water, whether it's at a beach or if it's raining. "Lucifer, you and the other angels haven't been getting along like you used to."

"We are getting along fine."

"You can't deny it. Ever since I told them about us, they have been shunning you. It's like you have to compete for me."

"I don't have to compete for what I already have."

"I don't want to be the rift between them and you."

"Sophia, I would endure the worst of pains for you. My love will never die. For eternity I will love you."

"You have my love."

"And forever you will be mine," he said.

It's funny how I am the strongest entity in existence, but his words comforted me. I didn't understand it. I was stronger than all of them, and yet with him I only wanted to be held and loved. I walked closer to him, and he put his arms around me. I placed my head on his chest and felt him breathing. I felt so warm; at that moment it was the most peaceful place on Earth. I just stood there in his embrace, basking in the glow. I didn't ever want him to let go. But then he did and took a step back.

"Look," he said

Suddenly he picked up his hands and made a fist. He clenched his fist tightly and pulled up. Then a mountain emerged in the middle of the river. The river ran right through the mountain. The water would fall from the top, straight down, and splash back into the base of the river. It was so beautiful; there was a mist that arose from the falling water, and within it you can see a rainbow. This is currently known as Niagara Falls. Besides the beauty of it, it sounds amazing. As the water splashed, you can just hear the natural motion of each drop if you concentrated. This became our spot.

"Or should I say listen?" he corrected himself.

I didn't know what to say. I just looked at him. "This is ... this is beautiful." The words sort of stuttered out.

"No, you are beautiful. This is just an expression of how you make me feel."

I looked at him and then at the waterfall.

"I want you to see how I feel." He said it so confidently, so strong. There was never a note of hesitation in his voice.

Then he grabbed my wrist and pulled me toward him. I looked up at him and stared into his eyes. I placed my hand on his cheek, and as I went closer, he came closer. It happened; we kissed. But it was a kiss like no other. When our lips touched, it was the spark of the most untamed and raw power ever. Our passion had built up, and our emotions were finally coming out. This touch was electrifying, and I, at that moment, was in a complete and utter bliss.

"Now I know what you mean, but too bad only you two get to experience it," Michael said as he walked in on us and saw us kissing. Within that instant, he turned around and fled.

As Michael ran away from me, I ran toward him. He stopped and looked at me.

"I guess the two of you are the only ones who deserve to love."

Before I could even say a word, he left and quickly disappeared into the forest. As I turned back I looked at Lucifer. With a tear running down my eye, making its way to my cheek, it started to rain. I ran toward the forest to find Michael. The more I cried, the harder it rained. I needed to talk to Michael. The look on his face killed me. I didn't want to hurt him; he was still my friend.

After about twenty minutes of wandering the forest, I saw him. He was speaking to himself, so I didn't let him see me. I just listened.

"Love, you will understand it when you feel it." He grabbed a branch from a nearby tree and started to break it up in pieces.

"I guess I will never understand. Was I cursed to live eternity alone, to watch as Lucifer loves, and stand aside?" He started to pace back and forth and then sat down. The look on his face tore me up inside. I knew what I had to do. So I headed back up to Mount Everest like before.

Michael was right; I didn't deserve to love while they just watched. There needed to be more of our kind. I realized what I had to do. I had to make more, but I didn't want them to be powerful nor immortal. I learned from creating the angels that nothing should ever be immortal again. So as a test round, I decided I would create two humans. I didn't just want to jump and create hundreds of humans unless I knew it would be successful.

So I stood at the same spot as before. With my toes in the snow, I looked straight up in the air. The snowflakes fell onto my face. I grabbed a knife and stabbed it in my heart. When I pulled the knife out, my wound healed; two drops of blood ran down the blade, hit the base of the knife, and then fell to the floor.

When the two drops hit the floor, they grew into two people. The same way as the angels grew, so did the humans, except they didn't have wings. Within seconds there were two fully grown adults lying on the floor—Adam and Eve.

When I brought Adam and Eve to meet the others, they were all standing there just staring at the humans. "This is Adam and Eve," I said.

"Where did they come from?" Michael asked.

"I created them; they are just like you and me, except they are powerless."

"What do you mean by powerless?" Raphael asked.

"Well they don't possess our speed, strength, or immortality."

"Why would you create them mortal?"

"I created them to live and love, and when they are done, they will pass on like the plants and animals do." I grabbed the hands of Adam and Eve and brought them closer to the angels. "Now I want you guys to teach them and protect them. Remember, unlike you, they can get hurt."

Before long, we taught Adam and Eve how to survive, communicate, and live. I spent a lot of time with them. I wanted to make sure that they were going to be safe and that they understood the dangers in nature. The more time I spent with the humans, the less time I spent with Lucifer. I still loved Lucifer the same as the day I created the humans. But I knew that I had to put aside my feelings and tend to the humans first. In the end, I knew Lucifer and I had all eternity, and I wanted to make sure that the humans could survive on their own first.

The most miraculous thing happened though; Adam and Eve fell in love with each other. This meant success; they were doing what I created them to do. They were living and able to love. I was so happy to see that this ended up working. Now I could create many more and this planet would be full of people enjoying life and enjoying love.

Lucifer got wearier of the humans and started treating them differently. He would take out the frustration he had from me on them. We spoke all the time and argued about how I was putting him second to the animals. He never liked to call them humans. I told him he needed to be patient, but it never made a difference. He didn't like the fact that I spent more time with them than I did with him and that they were able to enjoy their love. He claimed that all my love was for the humans and he wasn't able to enjoy his love.

Slowly his resentment for them grew, and one day it all came out.

Chapter 6

It was a chilly fall day, and the ground was covered in leaves. I went out to get some fish from the lake when I noticed it. I had a sick feeling in my stomach. I knew something was wrong with Adam and Eve. I rushed back to check on them, and what I saw broke my heart. Adam and Eve were on the floor, lifeless, and Lucifer was walking away with the most devious look in his eyes. When he saw me, he stopped walking and just stared at me.

"What did you do?" I asked.

"Nothing. I simply got our distractions out the way."

I ran over and grabbed Lucifer by the throat and threw him into a tree. When he fell I said,

"Distraction? They were innocent humans. What could they have ever done to you?"

"Done to me? They took my love away. You were always too busy with them and never had any time for me." He got up and looked at me. "I just wanted you back."

"I do not belong to you," I said as I walked over to the bodies on the floor. I started to cry, and as my tears hit the two corpses, they disintegrated into the leaves. When I blew the leaves away, they uncovered more humans. I created more humans from the remains of the first. More and more I created until there were about seventy.

"What are you doing?" Lucifer asked me.

"I'm creating more of them; I'm more powerful than you. Whether you want to accept it or not, there will be humans. Something deserves to feel what love is, because you will never feel it again."

"If you deny your love from me, I swear with every breath I take I will make sure no human will enjoy love."

The sad thing is that even though I was so angry with him, I still loved him. I still loved this man who just tried to ruin my dreams, because in a way he did do it for me. But I knew from that second we couldn't be.

"I love you, but I can't stand the sight of you right now." I made a swift blow in the air, and the ground opened up. There was now a crack all they way down to the core of the Earth. I walked over and looked into Lucifer's eyes. At this moment, my emotions were killing me. My heart was torn, and tears ran down my face. It started to rain, and you could hear the water sizzle as it fell down the newly opened crevice. Faster and faster, the rain became a storm. As wild as my emotions, the storm was getting out of control.

As hard as it was, I pushed Lucifer into the crack and sealed it. It wasn't enough to hold him for long, but it gave me time to get the new group of humans into a safe area. I ran and got the other angels and brought them to the humans.

Not too far away, a mountaintop exploded, and Lucifer shot out. As he flew out of the smoke and ash, he was only a skeleton. The lava in the core had burnt all of his tissue off. But within seconds his organs started growing back, then his tissue, followed by muscles, and last his skin. Once fully healed, he flew away. I told Michael to keep the humans safe. I had to finish up with Lucifer.

The land was turning cold, and the storm was getting worse. My heart was broken, and the land was turning as cold as my heart. I followed Lucifer to a mound of rocks, except the rocks spelled out something. I stood in the middle, and written in Aleos was "Forever you will be mine." Lucifer aligned the stones into this, which is modern-day Stonehenge. I fell to my knees and started to cry. Everywhere was getting filled with snow. My heart was confused, and I was beginning to scorn love, and then Lucifer walked out from behind one of the stones.

"I don't know why you hid; I can feel your presence," I said.

"I didn't mean to hurt you; I only want to be with you."

"I don't know what I feel right now, Lucifer. I need to be away from you."

"I still love you, Sophia."

"Goodbye Lucifer." I walked away from him. It was the hardest thing I had to do—to walk away from the one you love. My heart felt compassion and I understood why he did what he did. But I knew better, and my brain told me to walk away and not turn back. The hardest thing to do is to go against your heart. But I had to do it. I walked away and didn't turn back.

The land became so frozen; it's now known as

the Ice Age. It was the age in which my cold heart took over the land. It took about twenty thousand years for the land to recover, and not to mention my heart. In those twenty thousand years, the humans I had created grew into tribes and moved to different parts of the world. These tribes became civilization, and I just watched as they grew. One by one, each culture had created a god they prayed to, but unbeknownst to them, I was there walking amongst them, watching them as they lived and loved.

I never got a chance to see to Lucifer again. I remembered his words, "I swear with every breath I take I will make sure no human will enjoy love," because he stayed true to them. Every breakup was attributed to him. I could feel when he was around, and I knew what he did to the humans. He used his powers to tempt them and make sure true love would die. But a feeling like love couldn't die. Love could not be controlled, not even by me. I still loved Lucifer. Despite me wanting to see him, I never allowed myself to. I knew it was for the better, but there was still a part of me that wished I could just look into his eyes, at least one more time.

CHAPTER 7

Ring, ring … I turned and grabbed the phone, still half-asleep, so I put it upside down to my face before I realized and then fixed it. I could hear the traffic and noise of the city just outside my window.

"Hello?" I said.

"Good morning. This is your complimentary wake-up call. My name is Samantha, and I was wondering if you would like any breakfast brought up," the voice said in an extremely perky tone.

"Chocolate chip orange juice and pancakes. I mean chocolate chip pancakes and orange juice," I said, now trying to open my eyes while I stretched across the bed.

"One more thing Miss, with pulp or without?"

"Pulp, please,"

"It'll be right up." I could hear her scribbling on a piece of paper.

"Thank you," I said before putting the phone back onto the base. You know what I love best about waking up in the morning? Despite what may have occurred yesterday, today is a fresh start. I feel like I'm ready to go out there and do whatever comes to mind. There's a whole world out there, and I'm not even sure where I'll end up tonight.

I got up and walked toward the bathroom. I love room service; there is nothing better than waking up and having breakfast brought to you. When I got into the bathroom, I looked into the mirror at this massive brown bush of bed hair on my head. Standing there in mismatched pajamas, I brushed my teeth and then jumped into the shower.

When I walked back into the bedroom, I stood in front of the mirror. Looking at myself, I closed my eyes, and when I opened them, I was completely dressed. My soaking wet body, which was wrapped inside a large white towel with water still dripping from my hair, was now in a white button-down shirt and a black pencil skirt that came up under my bust down to my thighs. I grabbed my purse and pulled out matching sunglasses and looked down and was now standing in four-inch black pumps. Now after a few sprays of perfume and a touch of make-up, I was finally ready.

Knock, knock … Knock.

Room service was here. Excited to finally eat, I opened the door and watched as the bell boy rolled in a cart with a large silver cover, a glass of orange juice with two cubes of ice, and a miniature pitcher of maple syrup. Within a few minutes of him leaving, I finished my breakfast and was now slouched on the couch with an over-stuffed stomach barely able to budge. But I know I had to go. I'd been in New York awhile, and I was ready for a change of scenery. So I fought my lethargic mood and headed out the door.

Ding. I hit the bell for the concierge. "Hello Miss, I was just checking out of room 1526," I said as I handed her the keycard.

"How did you enjoy your stay?" she asked.

"It was great," I responded with a smile.

"Well, the cost of this stay is three hundred forty two dollars and twelve cents," she said, reading it from her computer monitor.

I looked into her eyes and whispered, "I already paid you."

"Oh, I'm sorry, Miss, here is your receipt," she said after hitting a button and handing me the receipt that printed.

"Thank you." I took the receipt and walked out of the lobby. Being god, I don't exactly have a nine-to-five; my time is occupied alleviating my creations. I don't have the time to earn a paycheck.

As I stepped out of the sliding doors of the hotel, I looked up at the sun and then pulled my shades down from holding up my hair. All around me was traffic and tons of people rushing to their destinations. There is no place with the hustle and bustle of New York City. You can hear the taxis honking, the people talking on their cell phones, dogs barking, and the construction workers hammering away. Despite all the commotion, the city was so beautiful; there is no place so filled with life. You could walk in the Amazon jungle, where you are literally stepping on life, walking through plants, and seeing all types of rare animals right before your eyes, but it's still not as alive as New York City. Here in Manhattan you can see a gothic man, a priest, a businessman, and a private school student trying to cross the same street. I guess that's why I love New York, its harmonic despite the mixture of such diverse individuals.

As I walked down the street, I saw a man dressed in a red suit with horns and a tail. He looked like an animated version of the devil. He was holding up a sign reading, "Apocalypse," and he was chanting, "God is a sham, the end is here." He kept lifting up the poster and repeating those words. Watching him challenge my existence struck a nerve, so I had to walk over and cease his actions.

"Is everything okay?" I asked him.

"No, I have to expose the truth," he said.

"What are you talking about?"

"I need to spread the word that the deity we pray to is nothing but fabricated," He was still holding up his sign.

"Who are you to question the authenticity of God?" I said, now with a serious look on my face.

"God is a mere fictitious character meant to instill fear in children. There is no factual evidence to prove such a being," he said in an overly offensive tone. Speaking to me in that tone just invoked a bad reaction.

"You wouldn't even know there is a god, even

if god walked over and slapped you in the face," I said while slapping him in the face. I had to make sure I didn't slap too hard so I don't break his neck. After that I just walked away, still agitated from that encounter.

After walking a few blocks away, I walked toward the street and waved my hand, so I could hail a cab.

"So where are we going, Miss?" the cab driver asked.

"Penn Station, my kind sir," I responded, slowly getting into a better mood.

"Oh, so where are we going to today?" he said, looking back at me through the rearview mirror.

"Honestly, I don't know," I said. I could see his expression change. He had this look like I was lying, but if only he knew that I really had no idea where I was going. It doesn't matter where I end up; that's the best part of the surprise. The great thing about Penn Station, besides the musicians and stores, is that this single station has so many different destinations.

As we pulled up to Penn Station, I stared at the people walking in and out. They were all so uniformed. It's like watching an army march, except in this army, every soldier is dressed distinctly from the adjacent soldier.

"That will be nine seventy-five, Miss," the driver said as he put the car in park.

I leaned over to the cabby and looked at his eyes through the rear view mirror and whispered, "I paid you, sir, and gave you a three-dollar tip."

"Oh, thank you very much, Miss; and have a good day," he said back to me.

I opened the cab door and stepped out. This was the first step of a new adventure. I could feel the energy coursing through me with each step I took, wondering where I would go. Hmm, Chicago, Dallas, maybe even Los Angeles. I had no limits, because from one train I could just hop on another until I reached a city that interested me for a while. I walked to the ticket booth to find out which train was leaving next.

"Excuse me, sir," I said to the cashier sitting down behind the glass.

He stretched over and spoke into the holes in the glass and said, "Which train will it be?"

"Which is your next train out?" I asked.

"We have a seven forty-two to New Orleans."

"I'll take it."

"That'll be one oh nine and thirty-eight cents," he said with this bored look on his face.

I leaned over and whispered, "I already gave you the cash."

"Oh excuse me, Miss," he said while slipping me a ticket and a receipt through a little hole at the bottom of the glass divider.

"Thank you." I took the ticket.

"You're going to want to be at terminal twenty-one. The train leaves in seven minutes."

I turned around and headed for my terminal. As I walked over to my terminal, I stopped at one of the various shops. I grabbed a banana-mango smoothie and two books for the trip. I was going to need something to do besides stare out the window for a thirty-hour ride. I enjoy a fine story, and these books had the words bestseller on the cover above the title.

When I got into the train, I walked into my room. For a ride this long, they give you a cabin with a bed to sleep in. I took a few sips of my smoothie and dropped my purse on the floor. I slid out of my heels, which made me feel short again, and pulled my sunglasses off, suddenly illuminating the room about three shades. I slipped into the bed, faced the window, and got ready to finish the sleep I would have gotten if I hadn't requested such an early wake-up call. I can see the other passengers walking onto the train through my window. I took a few sips of my smoothie and could feel the weight of my eyelids get heavier and heavier.

CHAPTER 8

After a nap and twenty hours of reading, I finally finished both books. The second book appealed to me in particular. It was called *The Lonely Road* by Erica McDaniel. Erica's book had a very different take on love; you can tell she was heartbroken. These were the last lines in the book:

> Today is a very lonely day
> The pain won't seem to go away
> And I can't help just what I say
> Because day by day I'm turning gray

The book concludes with the main character committing suicide. Erica has such scorn for love. It shows in her writing. I guess her heart hasn't mended yet, but everyone's heart eventually does. That's the beauty of a broken heart: no matter how badly it was broken, it always mends. People like Erica may have such heartbreak—she writes with a cynical tone—but one day she will find love again and her characters will live happily ever after.

It was time. I finally reached New Orleans, and the shaking of the train cars had finally stopped. I stood up and blinked. I couldn't be walking around New Orleans dressed like a New Yorker. I changed my entire outfit within that blink; my pencil skirt, button-down shirt, and black heels were replaced with a white camisole, jeans skirt, and red heels. I tend to wear heels because I'm very short and I don't like to be so little walking through a crowd. I know it's kind of absurd to have insecurities when you're god, but everyone feels insecure about something. I grabbed my bag and put my sunglasses back on and headed out of my cabin.

As I took my first step out of the train onto the platform, I caught a scent of the most amazing aroma. It was the smell of jambalaya. You see, New Orleans is a very special town; it's a town of flavor. You can only truly enjoy the beauty if you allow yourself to take in the flavor. The food, music, and people are all different; they flow to a different rhythm.

I caught a cab and asked him to take me to the nicest hotel by Bourbon Street. Before I knew it, I was pulling up in front of a beautiful brick hotel with a red-carpeted entrance and large black awning. As I walked through the large revolving doors, all I could see is "The Chateau" on the walls behind the concierge and a large fountain in the lobby. The driver took "nicest hotel" very literally. I walked over to the concierge and read his name tag, which read "Henry."

"Hello, Henry," I said.

"It's pronounced Enry, Mademoiselle," he said, correcting me.

"I'm sorry, Henry. My name is Sophia," I said, still pronouncing it with the H.

"Bonjour, Sophia, and what a beautiful name that is."

"I need a suite, preferably with a view."

"Smoking or nonsmoking?"

"Nonsmoking, of course."

"Qui, let me see what we have," he said before he began to type. Henry then paused and said, "Hmmmmmm," right when I thought he was going to say something. He put his pen in his mouth and began typing again. After standing there for about two minutes in silence, he looked up at me and smiled.

"Well, Sophia, it seems we have the perfect room for you, G604. I will need your credit card to put on the account."

I leaned over and whispered, "I already gave you my credit card."

"Oh, it seems everything is in order. I will have Philippe take your bags to your room," he said and then began to look around before asking. "Where are your bags?"

Holding up my purse, I said, "I travel light."

"Well it looks like someone will be doing a lot of shopping during her stay. Nonetheless, Philippe will show you to your room," he said, smiling as I turned around.

I walked over to Philippe and followed him to the elevator. Looking around me, all I could see were marble floors and mirrored walls. The molding of the ceiling was gold, and the ceiling was painted with replicas of the paintings in the Sistine Chapel. As I waited, there was a loud ding, and the massive elevator doors opened. I followed Philippe in, and after six floors, we finally reached ours. The halls were long, with dark red carpet and paisley beige wallpaper. I continued to follow his lead until we reached G604. He opened the door for me; as the door opened, the halls began to fill with the sunlight shining into the room from the windows.

"We are here, Miss," he said as he puts his arm out and bowed.

I walked inside and basked in the glow of the natural sunlight let in by the massive windows. When the door closed after he left, I pulled off my shoes, walked to the table and dropped my bag and sunglasses, and headed for the bedroom. I began to run, to build some momentum for the jump into the bed. Boom—oh the bed felt so good. After thirty hours of rocking from the train, it felt so good to be in a motionless bed.

I rolled over and stretched my hand into the night stand and pulled out the local maps, directory, and the menu for the hotel's amenities. I had built up quite an appetite; I usually have quite an appetite. I rolled onto my back and started reading all the pamphlets I found. After going through about five restaurant menus, I finally found the perfect restaurant, Firefly. Firefly was a Cajun restaurant known for its extra-spicy food.

I loved spicy food and was in the mood for some good jambalaya.

I got up and decided to change before I headed out to Firefly. I walked into the bathroom and took a look in the mirror; I blinked and was then wearing a little yellow dress and white sandals. I walked over to the coffee table to grab my bag and headed out the door. *The jambalaya better be spicy,* I thought to myself.

CHAPTER 9

As I strolled down Bourbon Street, I was mesmerized by its antiquarian beauty. Every step I took there was smiling faces, the most appetizing scents, and such upbeat jazz music. Each step held such pizzazz; it was like I was dancing. The sun was bright and gave me such a warm feeling inside. This was just so beautiful. I couldn't imagine how anyone would be sad. But amongst the people in the area I could feel a heart in pain.

I stopped and stayed silent for a minute. I could sense a woman in the alley between Sally's Trinkets and The Corner Stone Deli. I decided to go and take a walk and see what was bothering this woman. As I walked into the alley, I could hear children laughing and the dinging of trash cans. And when I reached the corner, I witnessed a very depressing sight. There were three children playing and their mother lying on a cardboard box. I walked over to her and sat down.

"Hello, my name is Sophia," I said.

"Hello, Sophia, I am Maria," she replied.

"What are your children's names?"

"He's Daniel, the girl is Anna, and the little one is Billy," she said as she pointed to each one.

"You have adorable children," I commented back. Unlike the average person, who wouldn't take a second glance unless it was one out of repulsion, I found the children to be adorable, despite them being covered in dirt.

"Thank you," she said as she tried to break a little smile.

"What are you doing on the street?"

"My husband developed cancer last year and lost his job. With the hospital bills and raising three kids, I lost my home. But sadly he passed away three months ago."

"I'm so sorry to hear."

"To be honest, I miss him more than my home," she said as a tear ran down her face, leaving the wet trail cleaner than the rest of her cheek.

While she wiped the tear off her face, I could

read her thoughts, and she was a very strong woman who never lost faith. Not one day had she turned to prostitution to make money or drugs to mask the pain.

"Maria, I'll be back," I said as I got up and dusted the dirt from the floor off of my butt.

I got up and decided to go and get some food for her children. I walked back from the alley and saw The Corner Stone Deli; I figured I could get some sandwiches and juice for the little ones. As I walked in, the hairy, chubby man behind the counter said, "Can I help you?" He had the raspiest voice; he should really quit smoking.

"Can I have four sandwiches? Turkey, cheese, lettuce, tomatoes, and mayo," I said as he got up. He walked over to the refrigerator and pulled out the cold cuts.

After about fifteen minutes of waiting, he walked back over with four sandwiches wrapped in white paper. "Anything else?"

"Oh yeah, I need three bottles of apple juice and one bottle of water," I said.

"Is that it?" he said. His voice now had an irritated tone. I'm not sure why he would be irritated. Usually people are nicer when they are trying to compete for business.

As I looked around him, I could see rolls of scratch-off lotto tickets hanging on the wall and said, "No, I need a two dollar 'Chance,' please."

"That'll be twenty-six dollars," he said after handing me the scratch-off.

I leaned over and whispered, "It's on the house."

"Don't worry, Miss, it's on the house," he said back to me.

"Thank you so much," I said, now happy despite the bad customer service experience.

As I walked out, I grabbed the lotto ticket out of the brown paper bag and waved my hand over it. I switched the symbols on the ticket. Now when Maria scratched it off, she would get a little surprise.

I walked back to Maria and sat down on the cardboard again. I pulled out the sandwiches and handed them to her.

"These are for you and your children," I said to her.

"What is it?" she asked.

"It's four turkey sandwiches. I hope you like turkey though," I said, while watching her remove the sandwiches from the bag.

Her hands shook while she unwrapped the

sandwiches. She called over her three children and gave them each a sandwich and a bottle of juice.

"Thank you, Sophia, may God bless you." If only she knew I am the one who does the blessing.

"It's my pleasure."

"What are you doing here?"

"I like to travel and help people along the way."

"That sounds like a lonely life."

"What do mean?"

"I mean no husband, kids or family?"

"No it's just me." When I said that I looked at her and thought about what she had said.

"You have such pain behind those eyes." This woman lost her husband and was now homeless, but she still had the courtesy to ask me about my pain.

"I feel pain for all humanity."

"No, you carry a broken heart."

"Maria, I have one more thing for you," I said so I could change the subject because I don't like talking about my heart. I feel no heartbreak because I buried my feelings too deep, and I don't want to bring it back up. So I pulled out the scratch-off and handed it to her.

"You got me a scratch-off?" she asked me with a confused stare.

"Yes, try your luck. You never know," I said while handing her a quarter to scratch the ticket with.

As she scratched the ticket, she clutched it like it's the only chance for her next meal. As she wiped away the gray shreds, she looked at the ticket and handed it back to me. "Here," she said holding up the ticket with her shaky hands.

"Why are you giving me the ticket?"

"You bought the ticket. It's a winning ticket, and the two million is yours." Even though she was the impoverished one, she was willing to give the money back to its rightful owner. I was right; she had just proved that her heart really was pure.

"No, Maria, I don't need it. Take it and start your life over again. Take your children off the street and instill the same morals in them which are of you."

"Are you sure?"

"Yes."

"Thank you so much," she said as she clutched my hand and began to cry.

Maria would buy a house in a few weeks and send her children to the best schools. Daniel would become a pediatrician, Anna would become a social worker, and Billy would become a human rights activist. The whole family would spend much of their life assisting other families with the similar circumstances to the one they endured.

As I got up and walked away, warmth overcame my body. It's a feeling I get whenever I help someone, because I know I was able to save someone who deserves it.

CHAPTER 10

By the time I finally got to Firefly, it was evening. Firefly was a restaurant and bar, with a very classic look to it. As soon as you walk in, you can see the old dark wooden floors, circle tables with a white cloth and glass top, burgundy walls, and a large brick bar in the back of the establishment. The whole place smelled like the kitchen, with fresh vegetables and the sautéing of seasoned seafood. There wasn't any hostess to seat you and only four waitresses who dealt with anyone in any seat. The waitresses helped everyone; I guess they split the tips as well.

I sat down at a table in the corner away from the busyness of the crowd. There was a live saxophonist playing on the stage in the back of the bar. His music held a strong, soulful tone, you could get lost in the blues. I sat down at the table for a few minutes before my waitress came. I already knew what I wanted, and the table had the menu opened up under the glass, so this would be simple for anyone.

"Hello, my name is Angie; I will be your waitress this evening. Can I take your order?" she said in a very heavy Jersey accent. It sounded like she said her name was Aingey. She didn't even pronounce the g in evening, and I could have sworn she said oider. Luckily for her I speak every language and I can read minds.

"I would like an order of jambalaya, and can you bring me a bottle of hot sauce please?"

"Any appetizers?"

"Onion rings."

"Drinks?"

"Ginger ale."

"It'll be right out." She then turned away and walked toward the kitchen.

As I sat there just looking around, I noticed a guy at the bar staring at me. Every two minutes he would turn back and look at me. He only smiled once, but besides that one smile, he kept avoiding eye contact. He was dressed in a black button- down shirt with orange stripes and the top button undone, exposing the little bit of chest hair he had. He wore stone-washed jeans, and casual black sneakers. I could read his mind telepathically from where I was, and I could see that he only had vulgar thoughts involving me.

Angie arrived with my onion rings and disrupted my telepathic connection. The onion rings were beer-battered, large, and fresh; you could still hear a little crisp when you bit them. I added hot sauce on my onion rings; it was like eating buffalo rings. For some reason, I love spicy food; I guess it's because the spiciness doesn't burn, it only adds flavor. Now another guy walked over to the one staring at me by the bar.

"Yo, Mike, where you went?" The guy sitting at the bar said to the newly arrived one.

"I was in the bathroom bro," Mike replied.

"Check out that girl in the corner, all by herself."

"Chris, you going after that?"

"Is that even a question?"

"True, are you going to use the 'stuff'?"

"Yeah I got it right here," Chris said as he tapped the pocket on his button-down shirt. He then turned to the bartender and said "Mr. Bar Man, can I get a cranberry and vodka?"

The bartender made the drink and slid it over to him. Chris then pulled out a little vial and dropped some white powder into it. He stirred it with the straw, tipped the glass to his friend, and said, "Cheers to a good night." His friend looked at him and started to laugh. As he turned around and got up, he looked my direction.

After about twenty steps, he reached my table and put the glass down. The sad thing is, I knew exactly what he just did, so that smirk on his face should be wiped off.

"I'm Chris," he said to me.

"I'm Sophia," I replied back.

"Sophia … I saw you sitting here by yourself and decided to bring you a drink. A pretty lady like you deserves company," he said while pulling out the other seat at my table and placing himself on it.

"How thoughtful of you," I said. I could feel the excitement running through him. He couldn't wait for me to have that drink.

"So, Sophia, what do you do?"

"I volunteer helping the less fortunate. What about you?"

"I'm a real estate agent. I don't mean to brag, but one of the best around." He then put his hand in his pocket and handed me a business card. It read:

Chris Mikena
Let Me Be Your Neighbor
HomeCo Realty

"Wow." I grabbed the glass and took a sip. The only thing going through his head was, *I'm gonna get lucky tonight.* Silly boy; if only he knew that I'm impervious to drugs.

Angie came back over with my food, and Chris ordered a drink for himself. I began my ritual of drenching my food with hot sauce.

"I can see the hot lady likes hot food," he said to me. Did he really think his jokes were funny? Now I could understand why he has to drug someone for any company.

"Ha ha, Chris, you are too much," I said to him. I was going to occupy him while I went through his memories and found out how many women had he done this to.

"So where you from?" Chris asked.

"I travel so much, I guess I would say

everywhere," I said to Chris. Actually, there was no place before me.

"I'm from St. James; it's only a few towns over," he added. As I went through his past, I could see he had a very loving family, which he abandoned after he started to make decent money.

"I've been there before," I said to him. But the last time I was in Louisiana the year was 1912, and this whole town was different.

"Really? I would have remembered a pretty face like yours," he said while tapping his finger on the table, and then continued with, "So what brings you back to Louisiana?"

"I'm here visiting a friend," I said. I thought might go visit Michael. I heard from Uriel that Michael lived here now, and I would like to visit him; it had been years since I'd seen him last.

"So where are you staying while you're down here?" He asked, like I would really tell him where I was staying. With all these questions, I felt like I was being interrogated.

"At a hotel," I said. By this time, I was almost finished eating. I was still going through his memories, and it finally came to me. What I had been looking for was twelve—twelve women. He met them and flirted his way until they trusted him, all while drugging them. Then he would take them to his hotel and take advantage of them.

"Which hotel?"

"Why do you want to know?"

"Um, I was just wondering," Chris replied.

"Can I ask you a question, Chris?" I said while I ran a finger across his hand.

"Sure," he said. I could feel his hand tremble a little when I touched him.

"Can you take me home? I feel a little sick, and I'm scared to go home alone," I said, making his heartbeat increase.

"Of course. There are a lot of crazy people out there, and I would feel a lot better if I know you got home safely."

"Thank you so much, but I just have one more question," I said as I moved closer to him.

"Sure," he said, smiling.

"Are you ready to get out of here?" I asked.

"Of course," he said, and I could see the excitement building up inside him; he was like a firecracker about to explode.

"Do you really think I am going to bring you to my room? Because there's not a chance in hell."

"What are you talking about?"

"Well, I know what you have been doing to these poor innocent women."

"I don't know what you are talking about." He was now trying to move his own chair away from mine.

"I'm no idiot; I'm fully aware of what you did over there next to your friend Mike."

"Are you a cop?"

"No, if I was I would have arrested you already," I said back to him.

"Well then I could care less what you think. I'm out of here. Bye," he said as he began to get up.

"Wait, I hope you realize what you have been doing is immoral and you should never do it again."

"Are you threatening me? Because this is not your business and I don't take well to threats." His voice was getting more aggressive.

"I apologize. You misunderstood what I meant. You will never do it again," I said back. I don't know who he thought he was talking to, but I didn't appreciate his tone.

"Watch yourself, woman."

I stood up and pushed my chair in and headed out of the door. I didn't look back because I could care less to see his face again. As I opened the restaurant door to leave, I heard a big thump, followed by screams. It appears that the chair Chris was sitting on broke. When he fell, one of the chair's legs was sticking up, breaking his spine with the fall. Now Chris is paralyzed from the waist down. I gave him a chance to change, and he mistook me for a fool; now he will never have the opportunity to do what he has done ever again.

When I got back into my hotel room, I changed into a large white T-shirt and fluffy slippers. Lying in the bed, I looked up at the ceiling and could remember the stars when time was new. Many stars have burned out since then, but I could still picture it as if it were yesterday. Back then instead of mattresses you had to find soft patches of grass. Instead of comforters, you had to use old animal skins, and instead of pillows you had to rest your head on flat rock. I love the progress we made.

I felt bad for what happened earlier with Chris. I think I may have acted harshly. But I had to make sure he didn't harm another innocent person. Even if it seems cruel, I have to make sure I protect my creations by any means possible. I never said I was perfect; I just try to do the right thing. That is what makes life so complicated; it's that there is no definite answer. One can only try one's best.

I turned and put the television on, flipping through the channels, looking for something good to watch. Somehow no matter how many channels you have, there is nothing on. I guess I'd make do with the news. The news makes me slightly depressed, though. I guess it's because I see all these problems. I wish I could be everywhere at once and able to help everyone, but I am only one being. I turned the volume up and began to pay attention to the newscasters.

"Now live to Angela Rivera in front of Saint Theresa's Hospital," the anchor was saying before the screen switched to a street cam showing a woman standing in front of the emergency exit of the hospital.

"Good evening, New Orleans, but it's not such a good evening for the Evans family." She was a young girl; you could tell she was a new reporter because of the way she held the microphone, and you could see that she was trying to hold her tears back.

"Tonight their five-year-old son was struck by a vehicle on his way home from the movies with his older brother, who is thirteen. When the cops arrived at the scene, it appears that the alleged driver was intoxicated. The boy was then rushed to St Theresa's Hospital. As of right now, he is in critical condition. The doctors say the next twelve hours will be most crucial. Let us keep him in our thoughts. Back to you George."

I grabbed the remote and clicked the television off. As I closed my eyes and concentrated on the hospital, I could see inside it. Telepathically, I could see into the Pediatric Intensive Care Unit and looked at the large dry erase board behind the nurses' station. It showed which patient was in which room. Evans, 416—now I just had to focus into the room. I could see this little body under a thin white sheet. His teeny arm was on his stomach with an intravenous tube running into it. His head was bandaged, and there were a few spots where the blood ran through to the top layer of the bandage. He had an oxygen tube in his nostrils and numerous machines monitoring his vitals. As I looked at this child, I had a flash. I had to go and see this boy tomorrow.

CHAPTER 11

There is no better way to wake up than to be awakened by the warmth of the sun's rays. It makes you feel like a bagel in a toaster oven. Speaking of bagels, I was in the mood for a cinnamon raisin bagel with tuna. Don't ask me why I like cinnamon raisin bagels with tuna fish salad, because I know it's weird. So I pulled the comforter off of my face and rolled over until I could reach the phone to call room service. I grabbed the phone and dialed zero.

"Room service?" I asked.

"Yes this is and a good morning to you. How may I be of service to you?" the voice said.

"I would like to have a toasted cinnamon bagel, tuna fish salad, and a club soda sent up."

"No problem, it will be there in a few minutes."

"Also, can you arrange some type of transportation? I need to visit a friend at Saint Theresa's Hospital."

"Sure, what time would you like the car to arrive?"

"In an hour please."

"See you in an hour then."

"Thank you." I said, before hanging up the phone.

As I got up, I grabbed my robe and then headed straight for the bathroom. The bathroom was large and bright. The tiles were white, and the shower could fit a whole football team in it. But my favorite thing about the bathroom is that the sink resembled a bowl, making it look more like an art piece than a sink.

While in the shower, I heard knocks at the door, so I jumped out and threw my robe on.

"Room service," I heard a voice say from the other side of the door.

I opened the door and watched as he rolled in the cart and uncovered my food. He then walked back to the door and stood there, holding up his hand. I walked over and gave him a kiss on the cheek, and within two seconds he turned redder than a McIntosh apple. His hand started to shake as he put it in his pocket and began to walk away.

After he left, the door closed, and I headed toward the food. They put the bagel and tuna fish salad separately; I guess this way they could charge me for two separate dishes. Luckily I wasn't paying regardless. I grabbed open the bagel and threw the tuna right onto it, and took a big bite, just like a great white shark and a blind surfer. That poor bagel had no chance.

Once I devoured my breakfast, I pulled off the lime from the rim of my glass and squeezed it into my club soda and took a few sips. I'm not sure what disguise I would go with today. I could be a doctor, nurse, or janitor. I decided I would be a nurse because nurses are often underappreciated for all the hard work they do. A doctor may have more knowledge than a nurse, but a nurse does the most dirty work, like taking your blood and dressing your wounds.

As I stood up, I thought back to how the nurses were dressed when I saw them last night. As I blinked my eye, I went from being in a robe to being dressed in a nurse's outfit. Of course, I had to wear flats. I couldn't wear heels this time or I would look more like someone's fantasy than their nurse. Grabbing the cart with food, I pushed it right outside the door so the cleaners would pick it up. I walked back inside and grabbed my purse and was ready for a day's work.

As I ran to the elevator, then down the hall and through the revolving doors, I saw my cab waiting there. I hop inside and said to the taxi driver, "Saint Theresa's Hospital." He nodded and started to drive. I could read his ID on the dashboard, "Muthen Ahbmindun." Sitting there I could read his mind and go through his past, present, and future. He had one daughter who was four years old, and he was having marital problems. He had very strong faith in Hinduism and would keep working hard for his daughter's sake, he would not divorce his wife; he's the kind of parent who would sacrifice his own happiness for his child's. It was all going to pay off, though, because his wife was going to leave him and he would fall in love with someone who deserved him.

I couldn't help it. I always end up tapping into someone's emotions and thoughts. Sometimes I wish I could just tune them out, but I can't. I'm always hearing people's thoughts, even when they're doing something as simple as walking by.

So I never have a moment of silence. I kind of miss those days. But it is what it is. I created all this life, and now I'm forced to forever watch over them. But I like it; I get to roam the Earth watching my creations love. Love is the most beautiful emotion, and I get to watch all forms of life experience it. It's the only thing that makes you completely blind. It doesn't matter if you're white, black, or green; it's the same feeling for everyone. Even though throughout time Lucifer had managed to conjure up ways to destroy love, it seems to prevail—most of the time. He's so scorned of love that he just wanders the Earth destroying any sign of love, but I'm always there undoing his damage.

"Oh, look, we're here," I said, all excited.

"That will be twenty-three dollars, Miss," he said back to me.

I leaned over and whispered, "I already paid you."

"Oh, I'm sorry; I'm a little out of it today."

"It's okay. Oh yeah, just remember to always stay strong. Everything will work out for you. I promise," I said as I opened the door and stepped out of the vehicle.

I turned around and walked through the main entrance. I saw a nurse passing me by with her ID dangling down in front of her. So I reach my hand into my purse and pulled mine out. I looked at it; wow, I loved the picture of myself on this ID. It would be sad if I created the ID myself and didn't like the picture.

I walked through the large white halls filled with portraits of all the philanthropists who financed the building of this medical facility. I went up to the pediatric intensive care unit and walked past the waiting room. I could see Mr. and Mrs. Evans sleeping. Mr. Evans was a pharmacist, and Mrs. Evans was an elementary school teacher. Both of them were immigrants who came here on student visas and worked hard to make it in America. They hadn't had much sleep, and Mrs. Evans had been crying all night. Even in her sleep, she was still sniffling and shaking.

I continued to the boy's room and walked straight inside. I grabbed his chart and began to read:

Broken Radius
Fractured Rib
Broken Ulna
Concussion
Coma

It's so sad when someone acts so careless as to drive drunk, putting their selfish actions before the wellbeing of innocent people. This is why people should think before they act; consequences are always greater than the action. All because this man wanted to drive drunk, this innocent child had to pay for it with his life. But this time it was different.

Well, little Kevin Evans, today is going to be your lucky day, I thought. *But from what I saw last night, you will give millions their lucky day as well when you develop the cure for AIDS. You will be the man who saves millions of lives.* Can you believe that this drunk driver would have killed him, and by doing so kill millions of people in the future? This is why a mistake can have tremendous repercussions.

I walked over and looked at him, just staring at his small fingers so still and lifeless. I picked my hands up and passed them over his body. A glow of light came from my palms, and slowly all his cuts and bruises started disappearing. Within minutes, he was completely healed. His eyes opened, and he caught a glimpse of me. He would probably think I'm an angel. It's kind of ironic when I help someone and they think it was an angel who saved them.

As I walked outside the hospital room toward the elevator, I saw a familiar face—this bright-eyed, strong jaw-lined face. His name is Lazarus, but you may know him as the Grim Reaper or Death. Contrary to popular belief, he is not a skeleton, does not carry a sickle, and never wore a black cloak. He is a very attractive man with a muscular body and dressed in a polo shirt, jeans with holes on the knees, and boots. He has this appeal that can leave anyone wanting more. He sees me and begins to walk toward my direction.

"Well hello there, Lazarus," I said.

"Sophia," he said as he looked me up and down.

"It's been a while."

"Let me guess, now I have to erase a name off my list."

"Sorry I had to intervene, but this twist of fate wasn't in his destiny."

"You're the boss; you don't have to be sorry," he said. While he was speaking to me, I looked at his stance; his frame was so strong, and his posture was perfect.

"So how have you been?" I asked.

"Things have been generally the same. Just work, work, and more work."

"You need to take a break, and that means a lot coming from me."

"Me, Sophia, when was the last time you thought about yourself and not the whole world?"

"Fine, I will go on vacation when you do." I said. Lazarus takes his job very serious; what he does is he collects the spirit after someone dies and brings them to the registration center. See, there are actually two realms on this planet, dead and living. The same way we all live is the same way spirits or ghosts live, in the same places as us. The dead realm can see ours, but only I, angels, saints, and psychics, or you may know them as witches, can see both realms. Once at the registration center, a spirit gets set up to have a "life" in the afterlife. So they can have jobs, houses, and even adopt children. They can actually have a whole new life if they wanted, or they can wait till their families join them.

"I guess a lot of people will have an extra week to live," he says with a little chuckle.

"That's fine; I'll approve the request."

"Well, a vacation together is a long time due."

"It will be sooner than later."

He looks down at his list and back up at me. "Well, it was nice to see you, Sophia, but I have to get going. There are still a ton more names I have to get working on. But it really was nice seeing you again."

"Don't worry, I'll save another life so we can do this again." He smiled and then walked away. After he left, Mr. and Mrs. Evans walked into their son's room. I was not too far away, so I could still hear what they said when they saw him.

"Oh my god, my baby is saved. It's a miracle," Mrs. Evans said, crying.

Mr. Evans followed with, "It looks like someone has a guardian angel." Angels get all the credit.

On my way out, I stopped by the bathroom. I walked into a stall and locked the door. I blinked, and before you know it, I was back in regular clothes, a nice pair of indigo blue jeans, a black shirt, and heels; I was so happy to be average height again.

As I walked out of the bathroom, I saw Lazarus walking out of another patient's room. Walking toward the elevator, I saw him looking at me from the corner of his eyes. I have a little attraction to him and he's asked me out a few times, but I'm not ready to date. I've learned my lesson, and I don't want another broken heart. So as my defense mechanism, I don't allow myself to love.

CHAPTER 12

When I got back to Bourbon Street, I stopped and looked at all the boutiques. It's funny how the clothes look so much nicer on the mannequin than they do on you; I think they should make mannequins with realistic bodies. But nonetheless, I love looking at all the different styles being displayed in each window. It's fun to see what other people design.

There's this one store named Bella's Boutique, which had the most beautiful dresses. They carried evening, cocktail, and party dresses. Every dress was different and flaunted a different part of the body. But there was this one particular dress that caught my eye. It was an evening gown with peach and yellow stripes, but not a bright yellow but more like a dandelion yellow. The colors had a pastel look to them, but the nice part was that there were rhinestones, so even though there weren't bright colors, the dress still had a shine. Once my eye caught this dress, I knew I had to go inside and try it on. As soon as you walk in the door, you can smell fresh flowers, because at every corner there are these big bouquets with bright flowers. Before I could take three steps, this tall, thin lady walked over; she was dressed in a business suit with an oversized nametag.

"Hello, I am Desiree, is there anything I can help you with?" This woman had a strange accent; it wasn't southern, but it was snobby.

"No thank you, I think I will just look around for now."

"Okay," She said while looking me up and down as she walked away.

Every other woman in the store was dressed just like her. They all had loud, stern voices, with a strong southern accent. I felt a little out of place while listening to them talk as I walked around.

"Oh Sugar, let me tell you what Richard surprised me with this weekend."

"Don't tell me, diamonds!"

"Well Mark got me this perfume that was custom made for my body."

"I know what you're talking about; I have body lotion like that."

But once I got close to the dress I had spotted outside, I completely tuned them out. I rubbed my hand against it and could picture how great I would look in it.

"Well let me tell you, every dress we carry is custom, so no one will have the same dress as you." I didn't ask for help, but I guess I looked like I needed it.

"It's beautiful!"

"Yes, my dear, it is. You should try it on. I bet it's perfect for you."

I couldn't help myself. I loved this dress so much. "Where's the fitting room?"

"Right this way." She walked over to the back of the store. As I followed her, I saw the group of women stop gossiping and stare at me. When I put the dress on, I came outside the fitting room and was looking for a mirror.

"This dress was made for you, dear." Desiree was nicer than she seemed at first.

"You think?" I wasn't sure how I looked because I didn't see myself in the mirror yet, but as I walked over, I could see the other women looking at me and giving me a condemning stare.

"It is because they cannot fit into a dress like this." Desiree made me laugh when she said that.

I went back into the dressing room and changed. I had to give it back to Desiree, because as much as I loved the dress, there was no place for me to wear something like this to. "I don't need it right now."

"Well it is on sale right now. Today it is twelve hundred, and tomorrow it goes back up to fifteen," she said while showing me the price tag.

"Thank you, but I'm sure." I walked back out the store. Wow, fifteen hundred dollars for a dress. That's why I'm glad I can just blink and be in it if I wanted to. I was getting kind of hungry, so I decided I would go to the next café I saw and have lunch.

While walking to the crosswalk to get ready to cross the street, this chill ran up my body. I'm not sure what it was, I hadn't had a feeling in centuries. I paused and focused on everyone around me. I could hear everyone's thoughts. I thought maybe someone needed my help or something. But there were too many thoughts coming in.

I wish I had the day off.

My kids are driving me crazy.

My brother needs to move out. He's getting to old to be at home.

If this dog craps here I will be pissed.

I think I lost my keys.

But I could hear a faint voice say, *Sophia*. I didn't get it. No one knew my name around here, so I didn't get why they would be calling me. So I stopped and started to try and listen again.

Honk … Honk

There goes my concentration. When I looked, there was this car pulled up in front of me. This car was about thirty years old but looks brand new and filled with four boys. They're not really boys. They're more like twenty-three years old, but to me they're still boys.

"Damn girl, wanna go for ride?" the passenger says to me.

I wouldn't even dignify them with a response. I'm not a dog; you don't scream at me through a car window. So I just gave them a dirty look and walked away.

"So what's up, come over here and talk to me." He shouts out. The guys in the back seat were whistling and making howling noises.

I was still getting this weird feeling in my stomach and a chill through my body, so I couldn't even waste my time thinking about what these guys were saying, I needed to figure out why was I feeling like this. So I decided to take a few steps back and ignore everything around me so I could pinpoint what was giving me this feeling.

"Whatever, it's your loss," they screamed at me as they drove away.

When the chills finally subsided, I held my stomach and looked up and boom. The car with the four guys crashed into an SUV in front of them. At that second, I knew it; Lucifer was here.

CHAPTER 13

I am not sure how I knew it, but there was no other explanation for that feeling I was having and then those boys crashing after hitting on me; but where was he? I didn't know if it's that I couldn't sense him or it'd been so long since I sensed him that I forgot how. But at this point, my stomach was getting filled with butterflies; if I burped, a monarch might have flown out. I knew I was not supposed to see him, and definitely was not supposed to want to see him, but something inside me wanted to.

I took a step back and wham. I turned around to see who I walked into.

"I'm sor …" It's him. I froze. I knew I wanted to see him, but I didn't actually expect to turn around boom, there he is. Tall, strong, with broad shoulders, he was dressed in a black suit, white shirt buttoned all the way to the top, bluish-green paisley tie, and shiny black dress shoes. When I looked at his face, he looked the same. His hair was cut neat, and his eyes were dark and deep like the bottom of the sea. He gave a little smile, which made his dimples pop out and made me want to melt. I was nervous, mad, and still a little excited; I was overwhelmed with all these mixed feelings.

"You don't have to say sorry, I liked it." He had this wicked smirk on his face after saying that.

"Lucifer."

"Sophia."

"What are you doing here?" I took a step back to put some distance between us.

"Hello would have been nice too." Every time he said something his dimples popped out. It had been so long since I'd seen him. I forgot how beautiful he was.

"So how you been?"

"Good, and you Sophia?"

"Great."

"So where are you going?"

"To get lunch, you?"

"Taking you to lunch. Let's go." He put his hand out as he said that, as to take the lead and for me to follow. But that was not going to happen. I looked at him and walked right past him.

"You seriously haven't seen me for centuries and just expect to take me to lunch?"

"How else will we catch up?"

"What are we catching up?"

"Lunch, Sophia … lunch."

"Okay."

After walking about two blocks, we ended up in front of this little café called Poison Ivy. The café was set up with tables and chairs for outdoor dining. The gate around the restaurant had a metal vine twirling around it, I guess signifying the name. The waiter sat us down, gave us two menus, and brought us two glasses of water with lemon. I picked up my menu when Lucifer pulled it back down to speak to me.

"Miss me?"

"No." I was lying a little; I missed him from time to time.

"Well I missed you."

"Oh?"

"Actually, I have tried looking for you for years, and I could never quite catch you."

"It's because I sensed you coming so I decided

to leave first." When I said that, he gave me a slanted stare.

"Oh really?"

"Of course. Do you honestly think I wanted to see you?"

"I know deep down you missed me too."

The waiter walked over. "Are you two ready to order?" he asked.

"Yes, I'll have a chicken salad sandwich with cranberries on whole wheat bread and a sweet tea with a lemon please." I folded up my menu and handed it back to him.

"Let me get a cheese burger deluxe medium rare with fries and a soda." Lucifer then flipped the menu closed and handed it back to the waiter.

When the waiter left, Lucifer sat up and looked me in my eye and started saying, "You know, you never should have kept running from me." He reached over and touched my hand. The second he touched me, I felt a little shock run through me, and I quickly pulled my hand away.

"So, Lucifer, what are you doing here?"

"I live here. I have a job, house, and even friends."

"And a girl?"

"I told you, despite it being thousands of years ago, you will always be mine."

"So what do you do?" I knew he was lying to me.

"I'm a lawyer, defense attorney to be exact."

"Oh, so you gave up ruining love for humans by any means possible such as turning them into monsters?"

"I would like to say that."

"So you're going to sit here and lie to me."

"Open your eyes, Sophia, I'm different now, I've changed." He gave me this serious look like he really had changed, but I still couldn't believe him.

"When I open my eyes, the only thing I see is the man who hurt me." Luckily the waiter was coming with our food. This way he could break the tension.

After about fifteen minutes of chewing and awkward silence, he finally broke it.

"So where are you staying?"

"I'm staying at The Chateau. It's a few blocks from here."

"I know where it is," he said while he laughed a little.

"Oh yeah, I forgot you said you live here now."

"So let me take you out. This way you can get to know the town a little."

"I know the town."

"When was the last time you've been here?"

"Years ago."

"Well then I guess being the kindhearted person I am, I have to show you around."

"Stop, you'll make me choke." Hearing him and kindhearted in the same sentence will make anyone choke.

"I'm telling you, Sophia, I'm a changed man."

"Men don't change, they mature, and since you're immortal, it should only take you another millennium or two." I gave a little smile after saying this because he started laughing.

"Just wait, you will see."

"I won't be here for that long, so I guess I will have to see the next time we meet up. It was nice seeing you. We should do this again. How about 4032? That seems like a good year." I began to wipe my hands on the napkin and got up to leave. When I pushed my chair back in, I saw him drop a hundred-dollar bill on the table before he stood up.

"What kind of gentleman would I be if I just let you walk home by yourself?" He said while pushing his chair in and walking toward me.

"One that respects a lady's wish." I tried to walk away, but he trailed me like a lost puppy.

After a ten-minute walk, we finally reached my hotel. I kept responding rudely to everything he said. What can I say? He brings out a different side of me. Despite my comments and slurs, he kept being nice, smiling, and complimenting me. I'm not sure what game he was trying to play, but I could assure you I wouldn't fall for it. I knew I wouldn't fall for it because even if my heart wanted to give him a chance, I knew better.

He walked me all the way to my elevator before leaving. As the elevator doors were closing, I saw him give me a little wink. I leaned back against the wall and thought about him—his smile, his dimples, and his wink. He was getting in my thoughts again and that was bad. As soon as I walked into my hotel room, I threw my purse on the couch. I walked into the bathroom and walked out in pajamas. I snapped my fingers and there was sushi, chocolate chip cookies, chocolate ice cream, and a stack of movies on the table. I grabbed the sushi, put in the fridge, and went back for the ice cream and stuck it in the freezer.

There goes dinner. Now time to see what movies we have here. *Sunshine Sally, Never Leave Me, In your Arms, The Heartbreak,* and *Tears From My Soul*; a bunch of movies that are all the same. Guy loves girl, girl leaves guy, and then at the end guy goes back and gets the girl for a happily ever after. What can I say? I have a thing for romantic movies. I guess we all want what we can't have.

It's natural to look at love and want that for ourselves, but I have come to the reality that I was meant to protect love and not to have it. I experienced it and got hurt from it. So therefore I learned my lesson, and don't need to relive that pain. But I hate to think that love is like an addiction. It's been so long and I need a fix again. I know I can't go back and make the same mistake twice, so the only thing I can do is to stay away. Stay completely away so there's no risk of relapse.

CHAPTER 14

After waking up still on the couch with the TV on, I rolled over and got up, stepping on the tray of soy sauce that the sushi was in. I needed a shower and a walk. I had a dream that Lucifer took me to the park and we sat by the fountain eating hotdogs while he protested his love for me, apologizing for the past and swearing to be a better man. Damn these movies. It had me dream something that will never happen. I just wish I could snap my fingers and have him like everything else, but the only thing I can't control is free will. So I am stuck dreaming of Lucifer being the perfect man because it will never happen. I have a better chance dying than him turning good.

I stretched and then walked to the shower. After

sitting on the bench in the shower and allowing the hot water to hit me for forty minutes, I finally got out and walked around in a soft, fluffy robe. I shook my head a little to make my hair all crazy, and within a few seconds, my hair was now set in curls. Today was a good day. I felt like going to church, so I grabbed the map from the end table in the bedroom and saw Saint Barbara's Cathedral, which was not too far away.

I dropped the robe and walked in front of the mirror and was thinking about what to wear. After a few minutes, it came to me—a white dress with red and yellow flowers. It was a little springtime-ish but definitely nice. It was August, so I could still get away with these colors. Now I had red pumps, so the only thing missing, which every southern woman wears for church, was a hat. Blink—a big white hat with red and yellow flowers on the side to match my dress appeared. It was a little much, I must admit, but you know what they say, "When in Rome."

Before walking out the door, I looked at the room. There was an empty container on the floor that had the sushi, ripped packets of soy sauce, dirty chop sticks, melted ice cream in a box, a dirty chocolate spoon on the table, an empty cookie wrapper, a sheet half on the couch, and two pillows on the floor. With a snap, the room was cleaned and back to brand new. I love having powers; I don't think I have ever cleaned by hand. I walked out the room, into the elevator, down the hall, and out of the hotel.

The cathedral was only a few blocks away. Within a few minutes, I was in front of this huge building that resembled a castle. It stuck out because much of the architecture around here had a classic American feel to it, and this castle-shaped building stuck out like a nun in a police lineup.

There were two entrances to the church that went around a big water fountain with angels pouring water on Jesus. The church itself was made from big gray stones and had a huge door in the middle with an even bigger window above it that was about twenty feet by twenty feet with a stained glass picture of Saint Barbara. I remember Barbara even before she was a saint. I am the one who turns every saint into a saint; I create a saint every so often when I feel mankind is turning too greedy and malicious. I pick certain people to live a life of virtue in the hopes of creating a change, not only a small change but a chain reaction to show everyone else the good and put mankind as

94 | Leo Anthony

a whole back on the path of righteousness. Saint Barbara was a feisty one; if you thought modern feminists were tough, then you should have met her. She even died fighting for what she believed in.

When you walked into the cathedral, there were tons of rows with benches stained dark chocolate and red cushions nailed to the middle for comfort. There was a dome in the front where the father was standing, which brought in large amounts of sunlight. As I walked in, I saw many people sitting with the Bible open, looking up at me as I passed them. I walked into one of the rows toward the middle of the church. Because it was a weekday, there weren't many people in each row. As I took my seat, I looked as everyone followed word by word during the mass.

I know you're thinking how ironic, me sitting in church watching everyone pray. But I like going to church, everyone goes because they want to. You get nothing out of being at church, so when you're there, it's out of the goodness of your own heart, and no matter whom you are physically, economically, or socially, when you pray, you are all equal, and too often people forget that. So to me it's a beautiful thing to observe. But there is one thing southern churches are known for: great gospel.

Toward the end of the sermon, this girl about eighteen years old got up and walked toward the front. She was little, not much taller than I, and looked very shy and timid. But when she opened her mouth, the walls were shaking. This girl had an amazing voice; she could sing instructions and make you pay attention. Looking at her, I could see her future. In about five years, after she has her first child, she will hit rock bottom and work in a record store. One day a producer will hear her singing while she cleans up the shop and he will sign her; and from that day money will never be an issue for her again and then everyone will get a chance to hear how beautiful her voice is.

When everything was done, I started to get the chills again. I knew it wasn't the Holy Spirit; it was Lucifer. As I walked down the center of the rows, I thought about him. I didn't want to see him, but yet I did. My emotions were even confusing me. When I walked outside, the sun had a strong glare, so I tilted my head down to block it, and I saw him there leaning on a small black sports car staring at me. He had on a white v-neck T-shirt, blue jeans, a silver watch with a big face, and boots. The v-neck showed the top of his pecks, and there was a little perspiration on it, which made it glisten, and his eyes were a little closed to block the sunlight as he stared at me. I walked over and looked him in the eye.

"You could have come inside; you know you wouldn't have burned when you passed the doors." I gave him a little smirk.

"I know, it's just the past few years I tried forgetting you, so going to someplace like this wouldn't have helped." Hmm, there goes response with a little sarcasm. I was waiting for one.

The pastor came outside the church doors and said, "Everyone, today is 'Feed the Homeless Day'. We will all be meeting up at Bayou Park. There is a picnic area already set up, so any volunteers should meet up there in about fifteen minutes."

I turned back to Lucifer and gave him a look.

"No." He answered me before I even asked the question. "The park is two blocks that way." He pointed due west and kept a stern look on his face.

"I thought you were a changed man."

"I am, but I wanted to take you out today, not feed a bunch of bums."

"Well I want to feed them, with or without you.

You do realize that we never had plans, so go do what you got to do." I turned around and started to walk away.

"Fine, I guess if the only way to eat with you is to eat with a bunch of smelly, dirty men, then I have to." He walked around me and stopped me. "But hop in the car, we're going to drive there, not walk."

"Fine." I gave him a big cheesy smile; I didn't really think he was going to be willing to spend his day feeding people less fortunate than himself. He was not the kind of person to do something he didn't want to.

When we got in the car, he started it and revved up a little. "Don't be scared," he said.

"I'm stronger than you. Why would I be scared?"

"Just buckle up."

"Okay." I giggled a little before I actually strapped the buckle on. I don't see the point in wearing a buckle when we can't die. Within two minutes, we were at the parking lot of the park. He got out and walked toward my door to open it. While he was walking around to my side, I blinked quickly and changed my clothes. Now I was in a white shirt, blue jeans, and heels. I reached in my purse, pulled out my shades, took my hat off, and my curls fell straight. Then I quickly threw my hat onto the driver's seat. When he opened the door, I came out slowly so that he could see I was now matching him.

"Wow, that's the fastest a girl's ever changed."

I couldn't help but to laugh at that comment as he closed the car door. Not too far away was the picnic area set up for the event. I walked toward the tables to get instructions. He tried to hold my hand, but I pulled it away. There would be no physical contact with the man I hate, or hate to love, whichever one you think. We got to the area, and there was a tall woman in a big t-shirt and loose jeans with her hair in a ponytail. She was holding a clipboard and telling people what to do.

"Hello, my name is Sophia, and this is Lucifer." I pointed to Lucifer.

"Hello, I am Margaret; I need two people for servers. Would you mind?" She wasted no time; she got right to the point. Well she looked kind of stressed, and her brain was working a hundred miles an hour.

"That's fine with us," I answered for Lucifer because I don't really care if he wanted to or not—he was going to help me!

"Well here are two aprons. Stand behind the tray of food. You will be serving the fried chicken, and he will be handing out the cornbread."

"Okay." I took the aprons and walked toward the trays of food. Lucifer trailed behind me and stopped to tie my apron.

"So are you ready to help me feed some people?"

"I live to serve cornbread." I started to laugh but caught myself. I don't want to show him that I was having a good time. Within two minutes, a swarm of bums came into the park. They all looked so different with the dirty colorful clothes they were wearing. We started handing out food; one by one they were coming up to us. Each smiled and thanked us for the food. It felt good helping them.

"You's a lucky man, gotch yoself a woman like this," this one bum with a black and a red glove on said to Lucifer. He was wearing gray sweats with holes that showed the jeans underneath them. He had on a T-shirt that was brown but once white and jacket with a missing zipper. I blushed a little when he told Lucifer that.

"Well you know you can have her if you want."

What a comment. I couldn't believe he said that, so I elbowed him and gave a dirty look.

"Sorry to burst your bubble, boys, but I'm no one's." The bum smiled and walked over to a picnic table by himself. After serving about fifty–three people, Lucifer and I grabbed a plate of some food and were looking for a place to sit. Most tables were full except the one with the guy we spoke to earlier, so we went and sat with him.

"Hi, I'm Eddie. Some might call me Crazy Eddie, but I'm not crazy." He scratched his head and smiled at us.

"Hello, Eddy, I'm Sophia."

"Lucifer here." He gave a little wave to Eddy and continued eating.

I turned to Lucifer and started talking to him. "Thanks for helping today."

"It's not a problem."

"I'm actually surprised you stood there for almost two hours and served food."

"I told you, it's whatever."

"So what are you doing later?"

"I don't know yet, why?"

"Good, because they're going to need some help cleaning up." I laughed as I finished my sentence.

"If that's your way of asking me to stay and help some more, then I accept."

"You two make a great couple," Eddy cut into our conversation and added.

"Thank you, Eddy," Lucifer said back.

"We are not a couple," I added as I turned and looked at Lucifer.

"Well, before gambling left me sleeping on a cardboard box, I was a couple's therapist. Let me tell you two, you got this spark between ya'll that would make a be-au-ti-ful relationship." Now I knew why they called him Crazy Eddy.

"I know, Eddy, that's what I am trying to tell this girl."

"Whoa, I know you're not trying to gain sympathy from a bum to get me to date you again."

"By the way, what's this?" Eddy pointed to Lucifer's wrist.

"It's a watch," Lucifer said.

"Can I have it?"

"It's a seventeen-thousand-dollar watch that I bought to match my car."

"Please?" Eddy gave this big smile, which was missing a few teeth. I gave Lucifer this look, which meant let's see what you do now. You were on his side when he wanted me to date you, now let's see what you do.

"Okay." He took off the watch and put it on Eddy's wrist. I couldn't believe my eyes; Lucifer gave up something of his to someone without personal gain. People had to sell their souls for a dollar to this man. I didn't understand it, but he did give up the watch and didn't display a regretful expression.

"It looks like someone is getting into a charitable mood," I said while I got up to get a garbage bag to collect the dirty plates, forks, and cups.

"What can I say? You're rubbing off on me," he said back as he picked up the garbage from the tables and threw it in the bag. We talked while we cleaned up, and before you knew, it was dark and we were sitting on the swings at the other side of the park.

I was sitting on one swing and he was sitting on the one next to me. We were both sitting sideways so we could face each other as we talked.

"Did you really not miss me?"

"I'm not answering that." I didn't want to tell him the truth.

"Well even though, I had a really good time with you today."

"I did too." I really did have a good time with him. It's hard to admit to myself, but I do like spending time with him. He grabbed my swing and spun me a few times and let go so I could spin back the opposite way. Then he got up, took my hand and pulled me toward the center of the park where there was a big water fountain. The fountain was a simple one, with only a few spouts of water shooting up, but the lights gave it an elegant look.

He came up behind me and whispered in my ear, "I still remember how much you love the sound of water." He hugged me from behind, and for that instant I felt so secure, so good. When I realized what was going on, I pulled away from him. He put his hand in his pocket and pulled out two quarters and handed me one.

"Aren't we supposed to use pennies?"

"Not when you're wishing as hard as I am."

He closed his eyes and threw his in, and with his lead, I did the same. When I closed my eyes, I asked, "This time let me not get hurt." This way I didn't wish for him and me to get together or not but simply that I not get hurt.

After the wish, he told me we should get going. It was late, and he has a busy schedule planned for tomorrow. I was actually cherishing that moment.

For a second I felt so vulnerable yet safe. When we got in the car, it only took us about three minutes before we got back to my hotel. He pulled up in front and put the car in park.

"Lucifer, I had fun today," I said, giving him a look of approval.

"Me too."

"It was nice to see you again; maybe one day we can do it again." I went to open the car door, but he pulled me back toward him.

"Just be ready for tomorrow," he said in a sly tone.

"Tomorrow?" I asked.

"Yeah, and dress comfortably."

"Why, what are we doing tomorrow?"

"Don't worry about that, just dress comfortably."

"Okay."

"Goodnight, Sophia."

"Goodnight," I said while trying to hide my smile.

When I got out of the car, I walked toward the revolving door. When I got inside, I turned around, and as the door revolved toward the inside, I was watching him drive away. When I got upstairs to my room, I felt different—a little weird I must admit.

Once in my room, I ran to my bed and threw myself in it, with shoes still on and all. I grabbed a pillow and hugged it. I could still hear his heartbeat in my head. I remember the first night we said we loved each other and I laid on his chest listening to his heartbeat. I will never forget that sound.

Boom

Boom

Boom

Boom

Like the tick tock of a clock, every beat was exactly the same. He is always so calm no matter what; it makes you feel so comforted to know he's not nervous and in control.

I couldn't wait to take a hot shower and have my body soothed by the hot water and my lungs cleansed with the steam. So I got up even though my body was drained and I just wanted to lay here and sleep. I dragged myself to the shower. Every time I take a shower, no matter how tired I am, I always get rejuvenated and feel full of energy.

As I sat there in the shower and got warm and cozy, I couldn't help to think what he had planned for the next day. I know he said dress comfortable, but I had to make sure I looked my best. It might be the last time I ever see him. It should be the last time I ever see him. I couldn't allow myself to get swept up away by his charm just to get hurt again. As much as I wanted to say I was over him, I was pretty sure I was not.

When I got out of the shower, I blinked myself into pajamas, not the big long fleece ones, but boxers and a tank top. I couldn't stop thinking about him—his dark eyes, dimples, tanned skin, and built body. I hoped I wouldn't dream about him again.

CHAPTER 15

What a night! I slept so good that I felt so refreshed and new, like a bracelet that was re-dipped in gold. I wondered what time Lucifer would arrive. I thought he would be there soon, so I decided I would get ready. I went to the bathroom, turned on the hot water, and to save time, I'd brush my teeth while in the shower. After a quick rinse off, I jumped out and tried to decide what to wear. He said dress comfortable, so I thought I would: red top, jean skirt, and of course my heels. If you're wondering how I can always walk in heels, it's because I don't feel pain, so heels don't bother me, and since it makes me taller, it's a win-win situation.

Within a few minutes, before I could even think

about breakfast, I heard the phone ringing, so I grabbed it and answered, "Hello."

"Hello, this is Katy from the main desk; we have a Mr. Lucifer down here waiting for you."

"I'll be right down." Since I didn't sense Lucifer, which meant my body was growing a tolerance to him, and that was bad because I shouldn't be getting used to him.

I ran to the elevator and took it all the way down. By the time I got to the front, I could see him there by the revolving doors, just standing there waiting for me with these sporty shades on, a hat that was on backward, an a-shirt, swimming trunk, and flip flops. If you're wondering how he can wear such a small shirt and not have his wings noticed, it's because an angel can retract his wings inside his back when they are not needed. When I finally reached him, he laughed and said, "Are you ready?"

"Yes I am."

"Didn't I say dress comfortable?"

"I am dressed comfortable."

"We are going to the water today."

"Well now I'm dressed comfortable." I blinked, and now there was a two-piece bathing suit under my outfit, so he couldn't complain. He laughed as I followed him into the car. Once we got seated and started driving, he put the radio on. After twenty minutes of listening to the radio, I finally heard a song I liked and started singing.

"From the moment your eyes met mine,

My heart froze like a moment in time.

Dum dee dum dee di."

But he turned the radio off.

"Hey, that was my favorite song," I yelled, as I went to turn it back on.

"If it's your favorite song, then what's the name of it?" I guess he was waiting for me to break the silence before he started talking again, which was so not like him.

"I don't know." It wasn't my favorite song. In fact, I had never heard it before, but I liked it. He looked at me and shook his head.

"Well I have to tell you the surprise," as he was talking to me, he exited off the highway.

"I know we are going to the beach." When I said that, he had a worried look in his eyes and a half-smile.

"Not quite. We are going to the swamp." He now turned off the main road onto a dirt road; it looked like were in the middle of a marsh.

"The swamp?" As I looked around I noticed we were in marshland.

"Yes, to see gators." He started slowing down as he pulled up to a bunch of trees near the swamp and an airboat. He went to the trunk and pulled out a basket. As I got out, I pulled my skirt down, because sitting there for so long made it go up my legs a little.

"Oh, you brought lunch."

"Yes and no. Yes it is lunch, but it's not for us." As he was passing me to go toward the airboat, I stopped him and looked inside the basket. It was full of raw meat.

"Oh great, you brought me gator feeding. Most people feed swans, even ducks, but you bring me gator feeding."

"Yesterday, did you not bring me bum feeding?" He was right. In all fairness, I shouldn't complain; also, I like gators. I did create them.

"True. Well it doesn't matter, I like alligators too." As much as I liked gators, it couldn't compare to him. He always loved the most dangerous animals. It's because just like him, these animals are misunderstood, and he has no reason to fear them. It's not like they can kill him.

He drove the boat about a mile out until we

reached an open area of water. There were four alligators lying next to a tree. He walked over to the end of the boat and started to bellow like an alligator.

"They're right there. Why don't you just walk over and feed them?" But before he could answer, I felt a wave that made the boat shake. When I looked at the water, a thirty-five-foot alligator came up and was about twelve feet from the boat. This gator was actually bigger than our boat.

"This is Sam; I've been visiting him and feeding him. He's kind of like my pet," Lucifer said as he pointed to the huge gator.

"I'm surprised no one else has seen him yet."

"Well most of the people who have seen him, ended up in him."

"Wow, he's as big as the ones you used to wrestle back in the day." Before humans and pollution, all animals were larger, and a thirty-foot alligator was considered small.

"You remember them?"

"Of course, you always loved spending time with them, wrestling, and feeding them."

"I taught him to play dead."

"Really?" I was so surprised that he taught this alligator a trick.

"No." When he said that, I couldn't help myself but to start cracking up. For a second there I actually believed him.

He started to open up the picnic basket and pull out all the meat. He had a bunch of chicken legs and thighs, but he also had three big whole chickens. He picked up one of the whole chicken and said, "I'm going to go feed him first, so just follow my lead."

I think he forgot who I am, so I stood up and pulled off my shirt and skirt and was now in my bathing suit and shoes. I walked over and grabbed the raw chicken from his hand and proceeded to the edge of the boat. Before I could take a step off the boat, I hear him say, "Shouldn't you take your shoes …" but before he could finish, I had already stepped off the boat.

"Honestly, did you forget that I can do anything you can, but better?" As I stepped off the boat in my heels, not a single part of my foot got wet; nor did I lose balance. I can walk on water, and heels don't make a difference.

"I didn't know you were so graceful."

"Oh yeah, well look at this." I walked over to the alligator named Sam and rubbed his head. He looked at me and made a loud sigh. "Aw, this guy is a big baby." I continued to rub his head.

"He's not a baby!" Lucifer got up and pulled his shirt off. Although he pulled his shirt off quickly, I saw it in slow motion, as the shirt came up and revealed each ab, one by one. I got so dazed looking at him with no shirt that Sam nudged me with his enormous mouth and picked his head up so I could scratch underneath it.

"Are you sure Sam doesn't think he's a dog?"

"No, he's a blood-thirsty monster." He walked over to us, also on top of the water, and grabbed the chicken back away from me. "Right boy?" he said to Sam as he threw the chicken in the air. Within two seconds, as the chicken was airborne, the massive gator opened his mouth, jumped up, and devoured it.

"You know a gator this big isn't going to be full from one measly chicken."

"I know, that's why I brought you here."

"Ha ha ha, very funny. Remember, I am more powerful than you, so keep on joking and someone won't have a spine anymore." After my reply, I had to laugh at him.

"That's not funny."

"Well it made me laugh." I walked back to the boat to grab one of the other chickens he brought.

"Sam is a very calm gator. You could lay on his back like you used to do."

"Okay." I decided to walk back over and feed Sam the other chicken. After Sam swallowed the chicken, I walked around him and laid down on his back. His scales were a little hard, but all in all feeling him breathe did remind me of how I used to spend time with the creatures, even before there were angels. I started to daydream about those days and closed my eyes, but when I opened them, Lucifer was gone. I had heard a little splash but I thought it was one of the other gators. I decided to leave him alone and close my eyes again.

Splash.

All I knew is that I was not inside of the nasty green water looking at Lucifer laugh, but I was wrong. He decided to go underneath Sam and jump out and pull me in the water. When I floated back to the top of the water, his head came up as well, still laughing.

"You know the reason I walked on top the water was so that I wouldn't be inside of it." I was trying to rub the dirty water out of my eyes.

"I'm sorry, I couldn't help myself." Still laughing,

he ran his hand through his hair, making the wet hairs stand up into little spikes. Even with messy hair, he looked hot.

"I'm hungry."

He picked his hand up outside the water and snapped his fingers. "Now turn around," he said.

When I looked back, there was now a table with two chairs, a picnic basket, candles, and roses.

"I hope you didn't forget about my powers."

"I didn't." He really surprised me; it had been so long since I'd spent time with someone else who had powers like mine.

"Do you want a violinist or is that good?"

"It's perfect the way it is." He really tried to make this special for me. I swam back toward the boat and climbed back up. As I stood up, I shook my body like a dog, except about twelve times faster, and within five seconds I was completely dry. Lucifer jumped back on the boat and squeezed the water out of one end of his swim trunks. No matter what men are, they are always sloppier than woman; we can try to clean them up, but they're always going to be dirty.

He pulled my seat out so I could sit down and then pushed my chair back in. After that, he walked around back to his chair, and as he sat, you could hear the noise of his wet trunks hit the leather on the chair. He went in and reached into the basket and pulled out two bowls, two glasses filled with ice, a bottle of iced tea, a bowl of buttered rolls, and a big pot of gumbo.

"Is that the basket of mysteries, because I don't think you could fit all that in there?"

"It's all about presentation, my dear." He gave a little grin as he went back in and pulled out one last plate of brownies. We ate and talked a while, but I had some serious thoughts running through my head and I needed to let them out.

"Why, for so many centuries, did you try so hard to destroy love?"

"Because I love you, and if I can't have what I love, then why should anyone else have what they love?"

"But did you have to turn innocent people into monsters just to break their hearts? You knew what was going to happen to them, but you still wanted their souls."

"It's because you don't know what you did to me when you broke my heart. I may be immortal, but it killed me inside."

"And you think it didn't destroy me inside to have to leave you? But you killed Adam and Eve.

They were my first two humans. I loved them. They had feelings."

"I had feelings, and you loved me; or did you forget that?"

"But for so many years after that, did you have to continue hurting innocent people?"

"I only wanted you, just a second chance."

"Well there will never be an 'us.' I told you we are done, and there's nothing you can do about it. But we can be grown up about it and stay friends. I mean, we are a few million years old."

"Whatever you say. I learned that I will take any kind of relationship with you, as long as it means having you in my life." Hearing these words come out his mouth made everything so clear to me. He did change.

"Wow, I didn't think I would be hearing you speak like that."

"You know I was never the monster people portrayed me to be." I am guilty; I helped people have such a bad image of him. I guess when your heart is broken; you take it out in different ways. Mine was telling people he was a red monster with horns who rules the underworld and is nothing but evil. But of course to me, after breaking my heart he was all those things.

"I know, but after what you have been doing to humans, can you blame them for the image they have of you?"

"No, but I told you I changed. After seeing you again in my life, I see things differently. I'm no longer bitter but happy. I see beauty not pain." Such beautiful words; I just hoped he meant it, because sadly enough, I was falling for every word.

"Listen, I don't mean to cut today short, but I have to get back to the office to finish up some paperwork. I have a big case coming up next week, and I need to be ready for it."

"That's fine."

"But tomorrow night we are going to the club. I want to give you a night on the town."

"I'm too old to go partying."

"Oh please, you don't look a day over a million." He said with his infamous smirk.

We threw the rest of the raw meat in the water for the other alligators and headed back to the car. When I finally got back to my hotel room, it was about three in the afternoon. I was not sure what kind of paperwork he had to do so late, but I trusted him. I couldn't believe I just said that I *trusted* him. I guess I had no choice but to trust him. There was no reason for him to lie.

CHAPTER 16

When I got back home, or the closest thing I have to a home, I took a hot shower and a short nap. When it was about six o'clock, I woke up and didn't quite know what to do for the rest of the night. I couldn't get Lucifer out of my mind, but I couldn't let this consume me. So I decided that I should cook to keep myself occupied. I don't really cook much, so I was not sure what I would make, but I thought I could go for some lasagna. I remember when I bumped into Raphael in Italy a few years ago and he made me lasagna. He made it from scratch, raw dough, fresh tomatoes, and all. Thinking about that made me realize how much we have all changed since we first lived together millions of years ago. We lived in harmony for a few centuries, and I kind of miss that. I think I should take a walk and pick up some groceries.

As I walked down the street, I saw this little grocery store. It wasn't like a supermarket where there are thirty aisles and you have to ask anyone with a nametag for help but a little store with fresh fruit outside, fresh meat hanging, and the nicest old lady sitting on a rocking chair.

While walking around the store, I saw fresh sausages and ground beef in the fridge, so I asked the lady for some spicy sausages and two pounds of ground beef. She handed it to me. The meat was wrapped in brown paper and tied with twine; I haven't seen meat sold like that in a long time. I put the meat inside my basket and walked over to the mozzarella cheese soaking in water and took a few balls out. I thought I would take some extra cheese because for some reason while I'm grating the cheese half of it disappears. They had many different kinds of pasta and flavors of sauce, so I decided to pick up the most expensive ones. I know it's not a good way to shop, but it's a habit that I have. I saw the jars of ricotta cheese in the fridge, and I grabbed it as well.

After gathering all the ingredients that I needed, I walked up to the counter and took out each item one by one. When I finished, the old lady walked over to me and smiled.

"So who's the special guy you're cooking for tonight?" she asked.

"I'm cooking for myself." That was a weird question to ask, especially when I came here alone.

"Food is the way to a man's heart, and a meal like this definitely shows you're trying to get to one."

"There is no man."

"Sweetie, I've been around a long time. Trust me, there's a man." I gave her this strange look because I know she looks old but there is no way possible that she is anywhere near my age.

"I'm actually all alone tonight, but I wish there was someone to cook for."

"Well keep wishing, god is great. He'll send you a prince charming." If only she knew.

"I'm no princess; my story doesn't come with a prince charming." But it does come with a prince of darkness.

"Your story didn't end yet," she said while placing each item into large paper bags.

"Trust me, there's no happy ending."

She leaned over the counter and said, "The groceries are on the house."

"It is?" I asked, because I didn't hypnotize her to give it to me for free.

"Yes, because this is going to be a special meal."

"Thank you," I said as I grabbed my bags and left the store.

That old lady was so nice, even though she was a little weird. But she had such a kind heart to give me free groceries when she didn't even know me. I wished I was cooking for more people than myself. As I got back into my suite, I put the grocery bags on the counter and started to unload them one bag at a time. When I was finished unloading the bags, I was wondering where I should start. If I cooked the noodles first, they would all be stuck together and hard by the time I was ready to put the lasagna together. I could either shred the cheese or start cooking the meat.

Knock ... knock

I had no idea who could be at my door; I knew I hadn't ordered any room service. So I rushed over and opened it, but I never would have guessed who it was. Lucifer was just standing there wearing a black T-shirt and dingy jeans, holding the biggest and most beautiful bouquet of flowers I have seen. It was an assortment of the most evasive flowers in the world. What a surprise it was to see him there. Maybe the old woman was right—at least partly.

"I'll do the cheese if you start the meat," he said as he looked over and saw the groceries lined up on the counter.

"I don't know, you might eat half the cheese before I get to use it." I knew I would. "So what are you doing here?" I added.

"I couldn't bear to be without you."

"What?" I didn't know what to say. I was so ecstatic to see him.

"I missed you so much, so I rushed through my paperwork and figured I would come here and surprise you."

"Well good, because I don't really know how to cook lasagna."

"Perfect, because at one point I was a chef." He walked in and handed me the flowers and walked straight to the bottom cabinets near the stove and pulled out some pots. I didn't know if that was a lucky guess or if he'd been here before. When I held the flowers, they smelled so good, like he sprayed perfume on them. I didn't know why he would have perfume, but they smelled great nonetheless.

I walked over and began helping him prepare the food. I had just finished washing my hands, so when I grabbed the sauce bottles and tried opening them my hands kept slipping. I picked up a paper towel to dry it off when I felt someone come behind me. I looked down and saw two hands opening the bottles.

"You know, many people believe that I have more than two arms, but I'm pretty sure I don't." I could feel his abdomen moving against my back as he laughed at what I said.

"I think it would be kind of cool if you had, say, eight arms."

"I think I can handle opening a bottle of tomato sauce by myself." Although I said that, I liked the attention he was giving me; I just couldn't let him know that I liked it. So I dipped my finger in the sauce and turned around and wiped it on his face. Right down his cheek was a red line. He then grabbed a handful of grated cheese and threw it on me.

"I know there isn't cheese in my hair." I then stuck two fingers in the sauce and threw it at him, flinging sauce on his nose, forehead, and lips.

"Fine, I don't want you smelling like cheese." He turned and grabbed a slice of sausage and threw it at me, hitting me on my forehead.

"Did you just hit me with sausage?"

"Yeah," he tried saying while laughing. But all you heard was a slap when I slapped him with a raw noodle as it cracked when it hit him then hit the floor. He then grabbed me and hugged me; I was stuck between the counter and him. I looked into his eyes and for that second I was lost. I closed my eyes and felt a shock run through my body, along with sauce on my face. He kissed me, and I hadn't felt that since almost forever. It had been so long I forgot how good it felt, but I knew how wrong it was, so I pushed him off.

"We better finish before all the ingredients end up on the floor instead of the pan." I had to change the subject because every bone in my body wanted to kiss him, even though I knew I shouldn't.

After we ate and were almost done cleaning, he asked, "What now?"

"How about a movie?" I said.

"Okay."

"Tears from My Soul?" I knew he wasn't going to be to happy watching a movie about a girl who

dies and her boyfriend kills himself to be with her. It's a classic love story and just what he's not into.

"A chick flick?" He gave me a look like he just smelled milk that expired two months ago.

"If you wanted to watch an action movie, then you should have had dinner with a man."

"I knew I went to the wrong room." He gave this confused look while rubbing his chin.

"G602 looked a little lonely. I saw him in the elevator earlier." I started to laugh at him when I said this.

"Fine, we can watch whatever you want." He walked over and hugged me. He rested my head against his chest and put his hand on top. I couldn't care less about the movie now—just keep hugging me.

When the movie was finishing, I was sitting on the couch, and he was lying down with his head on my lap.

"You know you're lucky," he said to me while looking up.

"Why?"

"Because unlike them, we are immortal, so we will have each other forever." He looked so cute looking up at me.

"Oh great she found the man she loved and

died, and I'm stuck with you forever." I laughed at him, making my legs shake underneath his head. But he just looked up at me with those puppy dog eyes and I couldn't help myself; he was just too cute. I leaned over and kissed him. It was perfect. When our lips touched this sensation ran through me, and so I continued. Sometimes being wrong can feel so good, and right now with the way this felt, I knew it was really wrong.

He got up and was now over me. I brushed my hand down his cheek, and he moved my hair away from in front of my face. I didn't want to stop, but I knew I had to.

"I think we should call it a night," I said to him. It took a lot out of me to finish that sentence.

"All right, walk me to your door." He got up and walked toward the door and I trailed; it's weird, this time I'm following him like the lost puppy.

"See you tomorrow." I said as I watched him walk out the door. I'm actually missing him even though he just left.

CHAPTER 17

"Sophia," a voice said.

I opened my eyes, only to see the shape of someone sitting beside me. I rubbed them to fully awaken and clear my vision, and to my surprise, it was an old friend, Mary. You may know her as Saint Mary or the Virgin Mary. I don't mean to break any general misconceptions that you may have of her but, she is a tall, thin woman with dirty blonde hair and hazel eyes, and a complexion that made her seem to glow; and yes Mary really was a virgin when she conceived a child. I placed a single drop of my blood into her water, which sparked life inside her, giving her the child she bore. I was so scorned of men after Lucifer that I didn't want her to go through what I went through, which is why I gave her an immaculate conception. I saved her the trouble of heartbreak.

Now Mary is a guardian. She oversees both realms and keeps order between them. Every saint, when they are deceased and are processed into the dead realm, becomes a guardian and keeps order between both realms. I'm not sure what I owe this visit to, but I'm pretty sure I would find out.

"Good morning," she said.

"Good morning," I said back as I sat up.

"I don't mean to bother you."

"That's fine, but I need to run into the bathroom and brush my teeth first."

"Okay, I will put on some coffee and meet you in the kitchen."

"Don't bother; I will have room service bring some. Would you like any breakfast though?" I reached for the phone and dialed zero to get through with the concierge.

"No thank you, I will be in the kitchen waiting." She walked out, so I placed the order and went into the bathroom. After brushing my teeth, I went and sat at the table next to her so we could have the conversation she came for.

"I haven't seen you in a while. How's everything?" I asked.

"Good and you?"

"Great, actually."

"Is that due to a certain someone who you should be staying away from?" Mary was never the type to hold back what she thought; that's what makes her a good friend.

"No, great because there's nothing to not be happy about."

"Okay Sophia, but as a friend I will say, be careful."

"I know you didn't come here and wake me up just to warn me about Lucifer."

"No, I actually need your help." She had her right hand inside her left and a concerned look on her face; I knew whatever it is she had to say would be bad news.

"Sure, anything. What is it?" I asked, but before she could even answer, there was a knock at the door, so I had to get it. The coffee had arrived, and a tray of fresh fruit. I took the plate of fruit and coffee off the cart and placed them on the kitchen table and locked the door after the bellboy.

"Sorry about that. What were you about to say?" I handed her a cup of coffee and placed the fruits in between us.

"There has been a disturbance in between the

two realms." She looked inside her coffee and then back up at me. "Do you have any milk and sugar?"

"Oh certainly." I got up and handed her some sugar and the little pitcher that the bellboy brought up with the coffee.

"Thanks, but back to what I was saying. There has been a disturbance within the realms. It appears to me that someone has been taking advantage of the spirits." She sipped her coffee and looked at me.

"Elaborate please." I needed to know more.

"There has been a strong dark energy within this area, and it has been intimidating many spirits to break the law and harm others."

You see, many religions, such as voodoo, works in a certain way. Someone who can see the other realm asks a spirit for a favor and usually has something to offer it. Then the spirit will accept the offering and complete the task that was asked. But there is a law that every spirit knows about: they must not ever harm anyone. If found breaking this law, they are banished beneath the depths of the ocean inside the Earth's core.

"Do you have any idea what can be doing this?"

"We know it's not any saints. I already paid four of the five angels a visit, and Lucifer has been too busy with you. But it does look like something Lucifer would do." I wouldn't put it past him; he had done so many evil things. It was hard to imagine him not being affiliated with this.

"So it's a psychic."

"Yes, but there are so many in this area, it's hard to pinpoint which one the negative energy is coming from."

"It shouldn't be that hard, Mary. Not many psychics are able to inflict fear into someone who's already dead."

"True, the other saints and I will keep looking. But we are going to need you when we find this person."

"I will find this person. You guys don't have to worry."

"When, Sophia?"

"This weekend, I will make it my main priority."

"Thank you."

"It's my job. No need to thank me. Consider it already done."

"So before I leave, let me hear about the two of you and why you have this twinkle in your eye."

She sat up, almost finished with her coffee and now picking at the fruit.

"Well, it's been nice seeing him."

"Is he going to continue being evil, making our jobs harder than they are?"

"I don't know. It looks like he has changed."

"Well, if there ever was a person who could change a leopard's spots it would be you, literally." Mary started to laugh at her own joke, which made me laugh.

"It has been an amazing week, but I still have to face the fact that it's not permanent and I will be leaving New Orleans in a few days."

"Well then I guess the only thing to do is enjoy it while it lasts."

"You don't think I am being selfish?"

"How? Since the beginning of time you have always put humans first. Now for a few days you have a chance to put yourself first. Just enjoy it."

"Okay, then I guess I have to get ready for tonight."

"All right, then, on that note I will leave."

"Thanks for the tip, Mary."

"Thanks for the coffee, Sophia." Mary then got up and pushed her chair in and left the room. Now I had to hit the road and get ready for tonight.

Chapter 18

When Mary left, I received a call from the concierge. They had a message from Lucifer; all it said was nine. So I went to the store and picked up a dress, make-up, bobby pins, and of course new shoes.

After I got everything I needed, I had about three hours to get ready, so I needed to hurry up. After a hot, steamy shower, I put my towel on and emptied all the bags onto my bed. I then pinned up the sides to give myself a muff on top and also to show off my new chandelier earrings I got. Then I pulled out a few hairs on both sides and trimmed it to have a little side bangs.

Next was make-up; I like to put on thick eyeliner and make my eye shadow smoky, to give that sexy-exotic appearance. You know I'm the one who taught Cleopatra about this look. Last but not least before putting on my dress is lipstick. Normally I like to wear lip gloss, but since we were going clubbing, I wanted to wear something more distinctive.

Now it was time to put on my dress and shoes, and a very sexy dress I might add. It's a very short black dress with spaghetti straps. The style looked like you took a black ribbon and went around my body about twenty times or like a very sexy mummy. I needed to make sure that my forty-million-year-old body could compete with these twenty-year-old girls tonight. I also picked up these cute shoes today. They have a six-inch heel. By the time I got my shoes on, the phone rang, and it was Lucifer, so I hurried downstairs to see him leaning on his car with that same old pose.

"Wow," he said. He was wearing a black button-down shirt with the sleeves rolled up and the first two buttons undone, long dark blue jeans, and dress shoes. He had his arms folded so you could see his forearm muscles.

"Thank you," I said while starting to blush a little. I saw his eyes as he gave me that up-down look, and then a little grin for approval.

"Get in, we got to get going." He then opened my door and closed it for me as I sat in.

Once in the car, he looked over at me, and when I looked into his eyes, I felt so happy yet sad. I was so glad to be with him, but deep down I knew this wouldn't last. He started to drive and said, "Are you ready?"

"Where are we going?"

"The Asylum!"

"The Asylum. You're taking me to an institution?"

"No, it's a club; actually, the hottest club here."

"Oh."

"Just be ready to dance," he said with a smirk.

"Just be ready to keep up," I said. When I looked down, I saw his hand on the shifter, so I placed mine on his.

"Oh really?"

"I guess you'll have to see."

"They play an eclectic range of music; I think you'll really enjoy it."

"Sounds like fun. I haven't gone dancing in years." It was true; it had been so long since I went out clubbing or even dancing.

"But first we are going to stop at a little café."

He took me to this little place called Teapot.

It's funny that they named themselves teapot but are known for coffee. Teapot has an art deco look to it, with red and yellow couches and glass cubes that were tables; there were even waitresses and waiters that brought you your coffee.

When I walked in, almost every guy turned around and stared, but to my surprise, Lucifer only placed his arm around me and walked to our table. Normally he would have gotten jealous, but this time he didn't seem to get mad. When we sat down at our table, we ordered our coffees and began to talk.

"You know, I can't seem to get you out of my head," he said. "No matter how hard I try, I only think of you."

"Then try harder."

"No seriously, these past few days have been amazing. Just to have you near me makes me feel so good."

"Me too, so let's enjoy it while it lasts."

"What do you mean while it lasts?" He had this concerned look in his eyes.

"Well we both know that however great this is, it's only temporary before you go back to your ways and I go back to saving the people you hurt."

"It's not like that." He grabbed my hands and

held them. "I really missed you, and I am willing to change my ways, all my ways, for you."

"You can't change; from day one you've had it out for humans."

"That's only because I didn't have you."

"Are you kidding me? You're the same man who finds the brokenhearted and cures them in exchange for their soul." I pulled my hands away because the coffee arrived. The coffee looked really nice; it had whipped cream and was sprinkled with cinnamon, almost making me not want to drink it so I wouldn't mess it up.

"That was then; this is now. I did that centuries ago. I'm telling you, I really have changed."

"Changed?"

"Look at me; you know in your heart that I am a good person."

"Lucifer, everyone knows that no matter what, you will be tomorrow as you were yesterday."

"So what are you saying, I'm a monster?"

I leaned over and pulled him closer by his chin. "Yeah, but you're my monster." Then I kissed him.

"Sophia, you know I wasn't always a monster."

"I know, I remember those days."

"Well, it can be those days again."

"Did you know that the average speed during rush hour is thirty-five miles an hour?" I had to change the subject; it was getting too intense for me.

"No I didn't."

"Well you learn something new every day." After about thirty minutes of talking and eating cheesecake, we left and headed out to the club.

When we pulled up, the building looked condemned, all except for the black carpet rolled out in front of the entrance. The building was made of stone, like the stones used to compose Medieval Prisons, and the windows were huge and barred. The ground around the establishment was cracked and unleveled, but that was where no one was able to walk; in front looked like a dirt road with a black carpet laid out. There were valets waiting for you, which gave an awkward look contrasting with the ambiance.

Inside was the complete opposite. The floors were black carpet, and the walls were gold. There were big red drapes that hung over the windows, lights that hung low from the ceiling that looked like stars, white lounge seats that went right around the room, and a bar in the center. The bar itself wasn't like any other I've seen. It was a large shark tank and was decorated with bones. The black lights made the sharks and bones glow. This club was packed, all except the VIP area, which was upstairs on another level, made of glass; this area wasn't really a second floor, it was only five feet elevated from the rest of the club.

We got a few drinks and danced. This club had some really good music. An hour went by with us laughing and dancing, not even caring about anything except moving our bodies and singing the words to songs we didn't even know. But then this song came on and it was different. It caught me off guard because I had never heard something like it before. It was a low, raspy monotone voice singing without any instruments. I paused and listened.

Bite me with the lust you have for me
I'm the apple of poison, you will see
Let my venom run through your vein
Soon enough you're gonna feel my pain
Running through your blood like an open sea
You can't fight the feeling, you belong to me
Feel the shock when I touch your hand
Like time in a bottle and drops of sand

The moment it hits your heart skips a beat
Like swallowing the sun you can feel the heat
Open your soul and let me in
A feeling this strong is only a sin
Taste my blood, for I am sin
Feel the power rush through your skin
Don't deny your lust for me
Hold me close and let us be

As I looked into Lucifer's eyes, each word hit me like a mole at an arcade. I never admitted it to myself, but I wanted him so much. No, I needed him; I needed him to be with me, to hold me and never let go. I stepped closer to him and kissed him. I knew it now—no matter what happened, I loved him, and me denying it didn't change a thing. As the singer finished with the lyrics, the song changed to African drums. I couldn't believe it, I loved African drums; I learned to dance to them when I lived with the Atawoo tribe.

I took a step back and began to dance; the drums were fast but not as fast as my hips. I started to vibrate my hips to the high-pitched drum and snapped them while they vibrated to the lower-pitched drum. The passion I have for Lucifer was being amplified by the music. I closed my eyes and kept dancing, even though I felt the ground shake a little. But then a hand grabbed me and stopped my movement.

It was Lucifer. "Stop," he said.

"What's wrong?"

"Look around you, all the glass is starting to crack, including the VIP section. The candles are melting, and the flames are getting higher. You're breaking the floor and the fish tank is leaking—a bullet-proof fish tank."

When I looked around, he was right, so I snapped my fingers and the whole place froze except for Lucifer. I snapped it again and everything was fixed, back to brand new. Hey, the club almost looked better than before. Within another second, as we began to walk out, the club unfroze and everyone went back to what they were doing. We got in the car and left.

Lucifer drove to the boardwalk, and we strolled along holding hands. It felt like a scene from a movie. When I looked at the water, I remembered the first time we proclaimed our love. I turned to him and placed my hand on his chest.

"So what happened back there?" he asked.

"I think I got to into the song." I couldn't admit that my feelings for him were coming out. It was an accident. I don't normally allow my emotions to come out like that.

"Oh."

"I'm sorry, I've been lying to myself, and been lying to you."

"What do you mean?"

"I love you."

"I know." He placed his hand on my shoulder and ran it down my arm. His touch is so comforting.

"I mean I love you so much, and although I try to fight it, I can't. I just want to be with you."

"I'm here. You're with me."

"But how long will this last?"

"Forever." He said it with such confidence.

"Nothing lasts forever." I've been around long enough to know.

"You're telling me this—the same woman who created life itself. You can have anything you want; now it's time for you to have it."

"I just want you to hold me."

He then grabbed me and hugged me, so tight I could barely breathe; but who needs to breathe? I just let myself go and relaxed with the movement of his body every time he took a breath. I knew I shouldn't have put myself out there, especially to him, but I couldn't keep hiding my feelings. No one should, no matter who they love, man or woman.

"I gotta get you home. Tomorrow's a big day for you."

I moved my face away from his chest and looked at him. "What do you mean?"

"Well, I have a big surprise for you."

"What kind of surprise?"

"A big one." His eyes lit up when he said it.

"Does it bark?"

"No, it's not a dog." He started to laugh and then said, "But I can get you one if you want."

"Then what is it?" I was never too fond of surprises.

"If I tell you, it won't be a surprise."

"Fine," I said, even though I still wanted to know what the surprise was.

When we finally pulled up to the hotel, he gave me a kiss good-bye, but I didn't want him to leave. "Do you want to come upstairs?" I said.

"I would love to, but no."

"Oh, okay." To be honest, I didn't expect him to say no.

"I want to, but I don't want to take away the

effect for tomorrow." He pulled me back closer and gave me another kiss.

"Okay, I'll see you tomorrow then, and it better be a good surprise." I gave him a smile and then left.

When I finally got to my room, I took a long, hot shower and put on my pajamas. I couldn't believe that I admitted to him that I still loved him, or to myself for that matter. It had been so long since I had felt this way after a date that I didn't want the feeling to go away. I had been out with humans before, but I never considered it a date because I didn't like them and I never kissed another man except for Lucifer. I don't think I would even feel a kiss from someone else, literally. Since I am immortal, I don't really feel things. You can stab me and I won't feel a thing, but Lucifer is so powerful he can counteract my powers, but never overcome them.

I didn't really get to eat, so I ordered room service and got a burger, fries, and a soda. I still couldn't stop thinking about him—the way he smiled and the look in his eyes when he saw me. He made me feel so loved, like I'm not alone in this world. I mean, I know I'm not literally alone, but there is no one like me. There are millions of humans and millions of spirits but only one Supreme Being; and Lucifer is the only person who makes me feel like I have someone else, someone who understands me.

I knew deep down inside that allowing myself to be so vulnerable to him might be the biggest mistake I ever made; but if he loved me as much as I loved him, then everything would be okay. What can I say? He's my monster.

CHAPTER 19

Yesterday was amazing, followed by an amazing night of sleep. I didn't wake up once, and I had a dream that Lucifer bought me a house and a dog. You never know, some dreams do come true. It was like three in the afternoon on a Saturday. I hadn't woken up so late in years; I thought I should turn back time a little so I didn't feel so lazy. But before I could get myself out from under the comforters, there was a knock at the door.

I jumped up and opened it to see who it was. When I opened the door, it was the bellboy with a large white box in his hand. The box was tied with a gold ribbon and had a card slipped underneath the knot. I took it from him, locked the door, and ran back to my bed. I wondered what it was. I knew the polite thing to do was read the card first, but I wanted to see what was in the box, so I tore it open and couldn't believe my eyes. It was the dress from Bella's Boutique.

I pulled it out of the box and held it against my body; it was the perfect size. How could he have known I wanted this? I didn't bump into him until after I saw this dress. I was so happy; I laid the dress down on the bed and opened the card and began to read.

Sophia,

The surprise has only just begun

Be ready for six

There will be a limo to pick you up

Forget about everything tonight

Because tonight is all about you

See you,

Love Lucifer

If this was the beginning of the surprise, then I couldn't wait for the rest. Now I needed shoes and a bag to match, but there wasn't one that was made for this dress. No problem; I blinked and now there was a peach bag and pair of peach pumps next to the dress. Hey, looks like tonight might be the perfect night.

The gown was exactly my size; you would have

thought that someone painted this dress on my body. Although I loved my shoes, they couldn't be seen because the dress was so long. You know, there should be more dresses for short people, because if I didn't like to wear such high heels, then the dress would be dragging on the floor; not everyone is built like supermodel. I think I'll go to a salon and get my hair done professionally. I haven't been to a salon in years, probably because I haven't been to any special occasions in years.

There was this fancy little beauty parlor called Melinda's Salon on Bourbon Street. When I walked inside I saw three women under dryers, two getting styled and one waiting to get started. I feel so normal going into a salon, waiting to get my hair done. Kind of like every other girl.

Melinda was this tall thick Hispanic woman, with beautiful long blonde hair. When she looked at me she said "I haven't seen you here before."

"I'm new to town."

"Well, my name is Melinda."

"I'm Sophia."

"So where are you from?

"Everywhere, my family moved a lot when I was a kid." I lied, it sounded like a nice memory to have.

"Oh your one of those army brats." She said with a smile.

"I guess you can say that." I said with a little giggle.

"So what brings you here?" Melinda said as she walked over to one of the ladies under the dryers, took out her rollers, and then the woman left. Then Melinda walked back to the customer she was previously working on.

"I need to get my hair done, my b...friend is surprising me tonight, and I think it's going to be a special night."

"Oh that special night?"

"No." I don't quite understand what she means by *that special night*, but I'm sure if the innuendo I think she's referring to is right, then it will be nothing like that.

After about fifteen minutes she was finished with her customer and called me over to her station. When I sat down she asked me "What would you like?"

"To be honest I haven't been to a salon in so long I have no idea."

"Let me ask you one question, what will you be wearing tonight?"

"Oh, he got me the most beautiful gown I have ever seen."

"Then it's an up-do."

"Okay." We continued talking as she did my hair.

After about an hour, a bottle of hair spray, and maybe thirty bobby pins, she was finally done. She spun my chair around and when I looked in the mirror I was completely surprised; I looked like a princess.

"It looks beautiful." I said.

"I know I do descent work, don't I?"

When I got off the seat I couldn't stop looking at myself in the mirror, I felt so pretty. We walked over to the register and Melinda said, "It'll be seventy five."

"I already paid you."

"Oh yeah, I forgot. I'm sorry."

"It's quite fine."

"Well knock him dead tonight."

"Will do." As I left the salon and walked back to the hotel I felt oddly different. Not like I had the world on my shoulders, but for the very first time I felt normal. I just wanted to go back to my room and finish getting ready for tonight. It's truly nice to have something to look forward to.

When the clock struck six, I walked downstairs to look for the limo. As I walked into the main area, everyone looked at me and the concierge told me how beautiful I looked. Sarah was now my favorite hotel employee ever. When I got outside, there was a large stretch limo and a man waiting by the door to let me in. I sat inside and saw more surprises; there was a bouquet of long-stem red roses and another note.

Don't ask where you are going

Even if you ask

The driver was instructed not to answer

I can't wait to see you

I miss your smile

Love,

Lucifer

After a thirty-minute drive, we pulled up in front of the most beautiful restaurant I had ever seen. The name was Spellbound. It was written on the top of the building, and the shrubs were pruned into stars. The entrance was over a glass bridge that had large Koi fish underneath. When you walked toward the door, a small Japanese man bowed for respect and then opened the door for you. Inside was just as beautiful. There was a table and chairs like a regular restaurant, but small private booths as well. Each booth didn't have lights but was illuminated with a chandelier of candles; each chandelier looked as if you went into ancient Japan and brought them to the future. The tables looked like you were eating on an oil painting; it was basically a glass on top of a painted table but yet so beautiful. On the table was a bamboo plant with a beta fish in the vase.

Standing next to the hostess was Lucifer dressed in a black suit with a black dress shirt and a peach and yellow striped tie. He matched me; it was so cute, even though it felt like I was going to prom. When he saw me, he walked over and put his arm out for me, and we walked together to our own booth. Although we were in a restaurant full of people, it felt like we were in our own secluded little world.

He placed the order for our food in Japanese and turned toward me with a smile and said, "You look absolutely stunning in that dress."

"You're not so bad yourself."

"So how you like everything so far?" he asked.

"It's perfect. How'd you know I love sushi?" I asked back.

"Because I love sushi," he replied.

"And you ordered what I wanted too." He forgot I also speak Japanese.

"Probably because I pretty much ordered everything." We both laughed at that, but the sad thing is that it's true.

"This place is beautiful. It reminds me of a restaurant I went to in Japan called Koi."

"I remember that place."

"You have been there?" I asked.

"Yeah, when I was looking for you," he said while he looked down at the beta fish in the vase.

"I knew you were around. That's why I left."

"You know, if you would have given me a chance years ago, I would've changed before."

"You're making me wish I would have given you a second chance earlier."

"You do?"

"Yeah, I really love you, and I'm glad we're together again." The food came, all kinds of sushi. There were Philadelphia Rolls, California Rolls, Salmon Rolls, Spicy Tuna Rolls, Eel Rolls, Shrimp Tempura Rolls, and Soft Shell Crab Rolls. Each set of rolls was on its own dish, along with a ginger in the shape of a rose and a cube of wasabi. The settings of the entrees were exquisite, and the food was just as good, probably due to the fish being so fresh.

He picked up his chopsticks and began speaking again. "So how do you like everything so far?"

"Amazing, everything is perfect. Every surprise tonight has been stupendalicious." As I said that he laughed at my fake word.

"Well the surprises aren't done yet." He had a little smile on when he said that.

"Oh really?"

"Just wait, the night's not over yet."

After a little while we were finished eating and we ordered green tea. He held my hand and just looked at me, and I admired this. I felt like our souls were merging into one.

"So when are you going to settle down and stop trying to save the world?" he asked.

"Never, my work is never done."

"One day you're going to have to think of yourself and let the world be."

"One day."

"What if I need you? When are you going to be there for me?"

"I'm here right now." I squeezed his hand as I said that, to reassure my presence.

"And I'm here for you and always will be." The

waiter walked over and placed two saucers in front of us, each with a fortune cookie on it.

"Read yours first," I said.

He cracked it in two and slipped the fortune out. "Happiness is closer than you think." He put his hand down and looked back at me. "Yeah, right in front of me."

"Now my turn," I said. As I picked up my cookie, he got up and started to dust off his clothes. I held the cookie in my hand about to crack it when he walked over to me. I placed the cookie in one hand, to not make a mess with crumbs. As I broke it, I felt something hard. When I opened back up my hand and looked inside, I couldn't believe my eyes. It was a ring, an engagement ring. I turned to look at him, and he was kneeling on one knee.

"What is this?" I asked.

"Since the beginning of time I have loved you, and for eternity I will. I want us to be together. This is a second chance for us, and we shouldn't let it pass us by. I can't wait for another five centuries to pass me by before I see you again."

"Uh." I was lost for words; I didn't know what to say. My heart was saying yes, you can finally be happy with the man you love; but my brain was saying no, you will only get hurt.

"I want your smile to be the first thing I see when I wake up and the last thing I see when I go to sleep." He picked up my left hand. "Will you marry me?" As the words came out his mouth, I was so happy, but this meant giving up being who I was, not traveling the world to help people but to live my own life. Could I really give up and let the world run on its own, abandoning all who needed me, all for love?

"Yes, yes I will." I handed him the ring, and he placed it on my finger, and in that second everyone in every booth started to clap. I knew I may have made the wrong choice, but it felt so right. Maybe it was time for me to be happy; I'd made so many others happy. I deserved it now.

He pulled me away from the table and kissed me, running his hand down my back. As his finger touched me, it felt like burning your arm, then running cold water on it, basically soothing a pain.

"Now let's get out of here." He then held my hand and led me out of the restaurant.

"What about the check?" I asked.

"It's already been paid for." When we got outside the restaurant, his car was there, started and waiting for us.

While sitting in the car diving back to the hotel room, I couldn't stop looking at my ring; the diamond was huge. I kept looking at it sideways and holding it up so every time we passed a street light I could see it again. So he turned to me and said, "So you like it?"

"Like it? I love it! It's absolutely beautiful."

"Put your hand down. You might hurt it holding five carats."

"Okay." So I rested it on his knee. "So where are we going?"

"Home."

"You can't call a hotel room home," I said.

"I know, soon that will be fixed."

"Will I get my dog?"

"You can have thirty dogs."

I loved my ring so much, but I knew it had to have cost him an arm and a leg; although he could always grow a new arm and a leg. "You know, I would have been just as happy with a small ring and spending the money buying clothes and food, then going to Africa and handing it out."

"We can do that if you want. We can spend our honeymoon in Africa helping as many people as you want."

"Really?" I would love to go there and help

some people, especially now that I wouldn't be doing that full time anymore.

"Of course, and we can adopt a baby while we're there."

"A baby?" In all my years, I never had a baby, never even raised one. I didn't even know if I could get pregnant. I'd never had the opportunity to find out. But I would love a child, one to raise and to call my own.

"Yeah, we can start a family; you can finally have everything you ever wanted." It was weird that he offered me the world and it made me feel so special, when I could have anything I want with or without him. It's actually kind of funny; I created the Earth, the sky, even life itself. But when he put that ring on my finger, I had never felt so complete—to finally have someone for me.

When we got to the hotel, he didn't drive to the front but to the parking lot. He parked the car and got out and opened my door for me. We walked to the hotel and into my room and he said, "Let's watch a movie, because tonight you're the girl who will have the happy ending." So we got cleaned up and changed into our pajamas. Well not really pajamas because he wore boxers, and I had on a big T-shirt.

He put the TV on and jumped under the covers, so I crawled in next to him. I placed my head on his chest and my hand over him and just laid there. I could feel his chest moving up and down every time he took a breath and hear his heartbeat. It felt just like it did the first night I slept next to him. It had been so long, but it felt the same.

CHAPTER 20

As I opened my eyes, I looked over and saw Lucifer sleeping. It was the first time in a long time that I was not waking up in an empty bed. So I sat up and looked at him sleep. He looked so peaceful just laying there. I leaned over and kissed his cheek. He then opened his eyes and looked at me.

"Morning sunshine," I said while I caressed his cheek.

He didn't get up yet but just looked at me and said, "You being the first thing I see just made my day."

"Good, because I don't cook breakfast." He rolled over on top of me.

"That's fine, because we got to get going." He

rolled off of me and started to walk toward the bathroom, so I followed him.

"What do you mean we got to get going?"

"We got to go shopping," he said as he walked into the bathroom, turned the shower on, and walked back out.

"Shopping for what?"

"A house."

"A house?"

"Yeah, a house. What are we going to do, live in a hotel room the rest of our lives?"

"Didn't you say one day?"

"Is today not a day?"

"Okay, but I'm picking it out."

"I wouldn't have it any other way." He walked back into the bathroom and started to shower, so I walked to the window and looked outside at the city.

Looking outside, I could see all these people walking up and down the street—women with strollers, kids with balloons, and couples holding hands. It might be nice to be one of those people. I looked back down and saw my ring. I was glad that I finally had the chance to be one of them.

When he got out of the shower, I jumped in, and we got dressed and headed out. On the way to go see the houses, we stopped off for coffee and donuts. When we finally got to the houses, it was beyond my imagination. I forgot how beautiful the architecture was here. Every house looked like the White House. We pulled in front of one that had huge trees and stone steps. As I walked up the stairs, I came up to two large white doors; the doors had glass in the center so you could kind of see into the house.

When I opened the doors and took a step in, I didn't know what direction to look at. Straight inside past the foyer was a living room with a wall of windows opened to the backyard; on the two sides of me were entrances to staircases that led upstairs. We walked straight upstairs and went to each bedroom, one by one. There was a master bedroom, two other bedrooms, and an office. The master bedroom had a lot of windows and a door that led to a balcony that oversaw the backyard and a lake that wasn't too far. The bathroom had both a stand-up shower and a tub. The other two rooms were similar but not as big.

The office was bigger than most I've seen in houses, but then again, everything is bigger down south. After a tour of the upstairs, we walked into the living room. To the left was a dining room, and to the right was a kitchen. The kitchen had an entrance to the backyard. When you walked out of the kitchen to the backyard, you were on stones, but a few feet out was all grass. The backyard is as big as a football field, and at the end is a lake. The lake is what connects all the other houses together. The neighbors had little paddle boats in their backyard, so that meant I would have to buy one.

As I stood there just imagining a dog running through the backyard being chased by a little boy and me screaming at him to leave the dog alone, I felt two hands on my waist. The hands made their way to the front of me, and Lucifer squeezed me with a hug.

"So what do you think?" he asked.

"I think if you don't buy it I will."

"You like it?"

"I love it. This house is beautiful, and the backyard is huge."

"The lake is nice too, right?" He shrugged his shoulders, and I could feel it behind me.

"Yeah, and you're not getting an alligator."

"What are you talking about?"

"I know you, and I know you're thinking about getting an alligator for the lake. But we can't because it will eat the neighbors."

"I'll train him."

"No. As cute as they are, I have to say no."

"Fine, but you better not get used to me always giving in."

"I'm marrying you, so you won the war."

"I know, but the battle was hard."

"Oh really?" I said as I elbowed him.

"Sophia, if you want this place, we can move in this week."

"Really? I would love to start shopping for furniture."

"After your ring, were going to have to sleep on the floor for a while."

"Shut up." No matter what, he could put a smile on my face.

"That's fine. Tomorrow after work we can go check out some furniture, and we also have to stop off at the real estate office to sign the papers."

"Okay." It's funny, in just one week I was engaged and buying a house. If you would have asked me last week what I thought I would be doing today, I definitely wouldn't have said buying a house. This man was moving faster than I did when I created the Universe.

"Are you sure that you don't want to see any other houses?"

"I'm sure."

"Then let's go celebrate with lunch.

We went back to Bourbon Street and grabbed some lunch not too far from where I was staying. We decided to get some crawfish. I mean, after eating Japanese last night, I thought I should enjoy some food that this area was known for. But then again, if I was going to be living there, I would be enjoying that food a lot more. Hopefully he didn't expect me to learn how to cook. It had a beautiful kitchen, but I didn't think I would be using it much. The only time I would learn how to cook is if I had a child, because then I had a mouth to feed. Lucifer could go out and get his own food if he was hungry.

"So how's the crawfish?" I asked him.

"Great, but there's a spot not too far from my office that makes the best crawfish around here."

"Well I guess we have to check it out since I want to meet your coworkers."

"My workers, you mean. I'm a partner of the firm."

"I forgot, Mr. Boss-man, I mean your workers." I was proud to say my fiancée was a partner of a law firm.

Buzz. Buzz.

His phone vibrated, he picked it up, read it and then placed it back on the table. "It was a text from the office."

"Oh, is everything okay?" I asked.

"Yeah, but remember that big case I'm working on?"

"Yeah."

"Well I have to go in and approve some paperwork."

"On a Sunday?"

"Sorry, but that's what happens when you're the boss. My signature is needed before any of my lawyers can process the paperwork." He got up and gave me a kiss.

"Bye," I said while waving to him, a slow wave, though, so he would feel bad for leaving me.

"I'll see you tonight. I won't be late. So don't go to sleep without me."

"I won't."

When he left, I realized that I had no money and no phone, so I couldn't pay for lunch or call him. If I was going to marry him, he better get me a credit card and a cell phone, because I didn't want to keep hypnotizing people. I used to have no choice, but now I do.

After lunch I went home and hung out for a

few hours. I sat there watching TV, kind of bored. After I'm married, I'm still going to help people. I thought I would do volunteer work while Lucifer was at work so at least I would be busy during the day and still helping people. What can I say? Helping people is what I do; it's like trying to get a fish to stop swimming.

Lucifer got back just in time before I fell asleep. I was already lying under the covers reading a book. The last book I read was about heartbreak, but this time it was about finding true love; I guess Lucifer made that much of a difference in my life.

"Sorry, Sophia, I got held up reviewing a case. I wanted to make sure the prosecutor doesn't have a chance tomorrow." He was taking off his clothes and folding them neatly.

"It's okay, as long as you got everything taken care of."

"I did."

"Now come to bed. I missed you this afternoon. I was so bored."

"Hold on one second." He walked over and pulled the comforter over my face and went back to putting his things away.

"When you left, it got me to thinking that I need a cell phone and money."

"Oh really?" He picked up his phone and dialed a number. Before you know it, I heard something ringing next to my head, so I sat up and moved my pillow and saw a cell phone.

"How'd you know I needed a phone?"

"When I was at the office, I wanted to talk to you and remembered there was no way of doing that. So I ran out really quick and picked one up for you."

"Aw, you're so sweet."

"And I will add you as a user to my bank account so you can have your own debit card and access to money."

"You're too good to me."

"You're going to be my wife. Nothing I do is too good for you." He turned off the lights and then slipped into bed.

"So what's the plan for tomorrow?"

"I have to be in court in the morning, so I probably won't be here when you wake up."

"Since you work, I'm going to start doing volunteer work."

"That's a great idea."

"Really?"

"Yeah, I think it would be great for you to still

help people. This way it's not too big of a transition for you to be settling down."

"You're the best." I leaned over and kissed him.

"Thanks, but I got to get some rest. I have to meet with my client really early to make sure he's prepared for the stand."

"All right, goodnight," I said.

"Goodnight," he replied. I snuggled next to him and fell asleep.

CHAPTER 21

I knew I had only woken up next to him once so far, but I missed him. I guessed I would have to get used to this. So it was Monday and I didn't know what to do until Lucifer got out of work. I thought I was going to take a walk down Bourbon Street and grab a newspaper and see if there was any nonprofit organization that needed volunteers around here, and since I was not married yet, I felt I was obliged to help any people I passed on the way.

I decided to take a shower, get dressed and head out. I changed from a big white t-shirt to a small white dress. It was not Labor Day yet, so I might as well take advantage of it, and like always, my shoes and bag matched. I also put on a pair of sunglasses; I always like wearing shades, even when it's night time. I headed out the door and made my way down Bourbon Street. I stopped at a stand, picked up a newspaper and went to a deli to sit down and read it while I ate.

I ordered a Po Boy Sandwich and a cup of coffee while I skimmed the classified section. Ad after ad was about hiring a computer technician or beginning a career as a real estate agent, but I saw a few that caught my eye. There was one about working at a kennel caring for pets from abusive owners, and one ad for a counselor at a women's shelter. I thought I was going to stop by the woman's shelter. I'd take the job and donate my paycheck back to the shelter every week; this way I would be helping in more than one way.

I hate seeing a woman who gets battered and abused; I try to help them whenever I meet one. So this job would be perfect, and my powers would give me an advantage. Lucifer would never attempt to physically harm me, because even though he is immortal, I was still strong enough to kill him. Nothing imaginable is beyond my abilities, so he wouldn't dare tempt me. I put the number for the shelter in my phone; it was nice to be able to say my phone. I was always so late with technology; I needed to start keeping up with all the advancements.

When I finished lunch, I went for a walk just to enjoy the area. I wanted to get to know the city I would be living in. Every store, no matter how small, had customers. That was what I loved about this town; it was always so alive. As I began walking down this one block, I started to feel weird. I was getting a tingling feeling. I could sense someone's presence, and it was an evil one. I had never felt such an evil presence as this since Lucifer. I tried to find the source of this energy telepathically, but I couldn't seem to trace it. It just came to me; this was what Mary was telling me about. I needed to find out who this was coming from.

As I walked down this block, I looked inside each store and at every person who passed me. Every time I walked past another store, I could sense the energy stronger and stronger. Suddenly I came toward the end of the block, and I saw this woman standing outside. She had the body of an Amazon and the face of a supermodel; standing next to her would make me look tiny. I didn't know who she was, but I did know she was the source of the energy. This woman was very beautiful, but the energy I sensed was so ugly. I walked toward her so I could find out more. When I got within five feet of her, our eyes made contact, and she smiled.

"Hello there, my name is Victoria Merloux," she said

"I'm Sophia." Victoria had black eyes, caramel skin, long black hair, and smelled like roses—my roses. She was about five-foot-seven, and with her heels on, she was standing at six feet and one inch. She had on a tight plain black dress and a necklace with a green gem in the middle.

"I'm the owner of Wicked." She pointed behind her, and I saw a small shop with the name Wicked printed on the window. "We read palms, tarot cards, and do potions and spells; whatever you like," she said.

"Really? You know, I can read palms too," I replied. When I looked into her eyes, I could hear her thought: *this little girl thinks she can do what I can. I'm what you see in the window and she's what you buy off a stand in the street. I can't believe she thinks she can read palms. If only she knew she's speaking to a high priestess.*

"Well let's go inside so I can give you a reading, and you know what? It's on the house."

"Okay, and maybe I'll give you a reading too."

This girl didn't even know me and she was already underestimating me. I guess we would see how powerful she was inside. If she was the one Mary was talking about who was manipulating spirits to do her bidding, then I'll be happy to take care of this.

When we walked into the shop, I looked around. The place was dark and cold. There weren't any lights on but candles lit everywhere. There were books and bones around the room and a tank with snakes. In the center of the room was a table with a black cloth laid on top and a deck of cards. The whole place smelled of incense and smoke. I sat down at the table across from her.

"All right, Sophia, cut the deck." She placed the tarot cards in front of me and I cut them.

"Okay." I did as she said.

After she laid the cards out, she began to read them. "So it says here that you are a traveler and walked the Earth in search of something—love. Then it shows for your love the devil card. This means that the man you love has broken your heart." If only she knew that what the cards were saying was that I was literally in love with the devil.

"You know what? I'm just going to skip the cards and read your palm."

"Okay."

"So just place your palm on mine and close your eyes."

I did as she said, and for a few minutes she stayed silent. Telepathically I looked at her, and I could see her squeezing her eyes shut trying to concentrate.

"Nothing, I see nothing," she said.

"What do you mean?"

"I see nothing, only white. Like if I was staring into the sun. I see no past, present, or future." I looked at her and she was getting frustrated. She didn't say anything, but her thoughts were loud and clear.

"Well let me try and read your palm then."

"Sure." She handed me her palm, but in her mind she was laughing. She didn't think I was as powerful as she was. The sad thing was she's on the bottom of the ranks compared to me. It goes psychics, then saints, then angels, and at the top is me. I guess I had to prove to her that I was not a fraud and she was not that powerful.

"Well I see here that as a child you loved stories about witches. You grew up in Nigeria and learned

Voodoo from a priest, but you surpassed him, becoming the strongest high priestess that he has ever known." I kept going, but as I was going, I was starting to get mad. Slowly I was finding out that she was the one causing the disturbance between the two realms. She was looking at me with a smirk and thinking that what I was saying is a lucky guess, so I had to go in deeper.

So I continued, "Now when you came to America, you were poor but gained money very fast by performing a few rituals. After you learned how to successfully communicate with the spirits and have them do exactly what you wanted, you decided to go pro."

"What are you talking about? You have no idea what you are reading. I'd prefer it if you don't make up a stories." She tried to pull her hand away, but I grabbed it, and her strength was no match to mine; if I grabbed hard enough, I could crush the bones in her hand.

"I'm only saying what I see. Now if I'm right, I see that you have hurt fifty-seven families and used your abilities to have thirty-two people killed."

"There is no way you see that."

"Now getting paid to harm fifty-seven families

is bad enough, but getting thirty-two people killed just gave you a ticket to hell."

"You don't know who you're speaking to. Now get your hand off me," she shouted in a very aggressive tone.

"Fine, but I'm not done giving you your reading. Now I see you are engaged. Let me just get a look at his face." When I saw his face I paused. I became frozen inside. It was Lucifer. This conceited, vindictive fool was engaged to the man I was supposed to marry. I was in so much pain, like someone shot me in the heart and was sticking a knife in to fish out the bullet. From what I saw, she and Lucifer had been dating for three years and engaged for one.

"So where is your fiancé?" I asked.

"He's been away on a business meeting. It's for one week, and he will be here tomorrow. Why are you asking?"

"Forget about him. I'm going to start reading your future." I would not blame her for being engaged to Lucifer; I would blame him. No man takes me for a fool. If he didn't know that then, he would find out when I was finished with her. But I understood why he fell for her; she was just as evil as he was.

"Now you will stop practicing voodoo to harm people or what you have done will come back to haunt you."

"Are you threatening me?" Her eyes were now red and she was standing with her arms folded, expressing her aggression openly.

"No, I'm simply telling you your future." I hoped she realized that I was not afraid of her; there was nothing she could do to harm me.

"You listen to me; you have no idea who you're speaking to. I have mastered my abilities and I laugh at death. I am warning you, I don't have a conscience."

"Sweetie, listen to me. Your abilities are a mere parlor trick, and I hired death. Before I get upset, I just want you to promise you will not harm anyone else."

"You dare threaten me?" She held out her hands and closed her eyes and chanted, "Hum Takar Omere Dia," which means, "I summon the dead." All of a sudden thirteen spirits surrounded me, spirits of warriors who died during battle.

"Are you that stupid?"

"I told you I have no problem killing you. No one threatens me. I am the closest thing to god."

Victoria needed to get her facts straight; she was the furthest thing from me.

"Hello." I looked at the spirits, and when they got a good look at my face, they went from an attack stance to dropping on their knees and bowing.

"What the hell is going on here? Why are they bowing; and to you?"

"Because unlike you, they know better."

"They're dead. There is no reason they should fear you."

"There are worse things than dying."

"Well if they don't kill you, I will." She ran over to her book stand and grabbed an ancient dagger used to do sacrifices. She ran over and stabbed me. Of course I didn't move, because that dagger wasn't going to do anything to me; so when the blade hit my skin, it broke.

"You dare try and kill me?" Now I was pacing back and forth. "Now for the many innocent people you've hurt, you will feel what you put them through."

"God will forgive me," she said as she rolled her eyes.

I snapped my fingers, and the chair flew from behind her and she fell onto it, and all of a sudden her hands and feet were tied down. So I walked over to her and leaned next to her face and said, "Your god is a vengeful one." With that being said, I walked back to the table, which was only about two feet away, and sat on it with my legs crossed.

"Now remember when witches were burned at the stake? Well, all those witches were innocent women; they were only women who had the ability to see both my realms, just like you. Those men who burnt them felt it in the dead realm, because what you do to someone never gets forgotten. But they had one thing right: I do burn things. Well, when I do it, it's a little different. It's called a holy fire. A holy fire can pass through a whole town but only burn what's evil, and so a witch would be completely fine unless she had an evil heart. See, a holy fire doesn't affect anything that isn't evil. You will see that now. So the chair you're sitting in, the ropes tying you down, and the shop we're in will not be touched at all, but let's see what happens to you."

I snapped my finger, and Victoria was lit on fire. She started to scream as she was burning; her tears sizzled as they hit the fire. Within a few minutes after the shrieking had finished, this beautiful woman who was sitting there was nothing but ash on the chair. So I snapped my fingers again and she appeared in front of me, except now she was a spirit.

"So, Victoria, how did that feel?"

"What did you do to me, you heartless creature?" She looked furious, but it didn't matter; she was dead. Now all the spirits she summoned were surrounding her.

"I only did to you what you did to others. Take a look around you. These are the spirits you tried to manipulate into doing your bidding, but now you're in their realm. Ask them for help."

"I'm not afraid of them."

"Are you still going to try me, I mean honestly, Victoria? Now turn around and look at your ashes on the chair." She turned and looked at it and started crying. "Why are you crying? You didn't cry when you were causing the pain. Don't worry, I could leave you dead so that the spirits could finish tormenting you in the dead realm, but I don't think that's harsh enough."

"Harsh enough?" she asked.

"No." I snapped my fingers, and she was back to life. "Boys, I think you should get back to whatever you were doing before she summoned you; and don't be upset, sooner or later she will be dead and you can torture her for eternity."

"Do you know what it feels like to be burned alive?" she said to me, still with tears in her eyes.

"No, probably because I don't feel pain." That was a lie, though, because right then I was going through more pain than she was. *Wait till I'm done with her and I catch Lucifer,* I thought. A broken heart is worse than a burn. Emotional pain trumps physical pain; you can't take a pain killer for a broken heart.

"That wasn't just, what you did was cruel." Now she wasn't sounding to condescending anymore, in fact I sensed a hint of fear in her voice.

"Well I'm not done yet. With the snap of a finger your bank account is now empty, your shop is foreclosed, house repossessed by the bank, car crashed, and your dog ran away. Now you have nothing and will be forced to start from scratch. But think twice if you think voodoo is going to help you like it did last time. Voodoo may do good, but it won't work for you. You're now blacklisted in the dead realm; in fact, most of them can't wait to get their hands on you."

"I can't believe you do this to people. I know what you are, and what you just did is wrong. You're supposed to be benevolent, not destructive."

"You're wrong. I save people all the time, but

I punish as well. I will not have innocent people suffer by the hands of monsters like you. I will make the evil hearted feel what they inflict, and I will reward the ones who live their lives caring for others. To you I may be cruel, but who gave you the right to do what you did? I created you, and I have the right to take you out if I want. Never take your eyes and pass me again, because I am all powerful!" I hopped off the table and walked toward the door.

"Before I leave, if you change your ways and decide to live where you help others and show compassion, everything will come back. I'm not forcing you to be homeless forever. If you open your heart, if you have one, you will get back everything you lost," I said to her.

"I'd rather be nothing; I will never be what you want me to be. So on the street I shall sleep, but I will live the way I please."

"Very well, now get out of this building. You can get arrested for trespassing." I opened the door and left. As I walked outside, I couldn't hold it in anymore. The tears started to pour out, and I could barely stand. I ran over to a taxi that was passing and jumped inside. I didn't even speak to him; I told him to drive telepathically. As I looked out the window, I could see the skies were getting dark. My eyes were redder than a cherry, and the tears were just pouring out.

I loved this man; I gave up everything for him. I was willing to stop doing the very thing I lived for, just for him. I was going to stop helping people and let whatever happen, happen just to be with him. But he proved me a fool; I knew better too. I guess your heart can be wrong, but why is it that we are blind when we are in love? I know I shouldn't be asking these questions, but it comes down to this: no one, no matter who, can control their heart. We are just helpless to our emotions.

I am dead inside; he killed me by breaking my heart. Not only once have I allowed myself to be hurt by him but twice. I don't feel pain, but right now it hurts so much I can barely breathe. I ensure you that he will feel what I feel, one way or another.

CHAPTER 22

As mad as I was, tears still falling, I picked up my phone and called him. There were only two numbers stored, so it was easy to tell which one was his. Right now I belonged at that shelter, so it didn't even matter which number I called.

Ring.

Ring.

The phone rang, and he finally answered. I couldn't talk. I was only crying. He said, "Hello, Hello. Sophia, what's wrong. I can hear you. It sounds like you're crying. What's wrong?"

"Hello," I said. This was the maddest I had ever spoken. My voice was strong enough to crack the windows in the cab.

"Sophia, what's wrong? Why do I hear you crying?"

"Meet me by the pier, now," I said as I quivered.

"I can't. It will take me at least twenty minutes to get there with traffic."

"Fly." I was so mad; I couldn't even speak to him.

"What, you want me to fly there?" He sounded so surprised, like he didn't have wings.

"Be there, now." Click. I hung up the phone and crushed it in my hand. It went from a cell phone to dust.

When I reached the boardwalk, the taxi left, and I began to walk toward the pier, the same pier we were at that night. The whole place was windy now. There was garbage being swept away by the wind, and all the clouds were black in the sky. As my tears hit the floor, the clouds started to rain, and the more I sobbed, the harder it poured. I don't mean for it to rain, but I couldn't help my emotions right now. When I finally reached the pier, I saw something swooping down from the sky. It was Lucifer.

"What's wrong, Sophia?" He walked toward me with his arms open, as if to hug me for comfort.

I pushed him away, but it was hard enough to throw him about thirty feet away. His wings were still out, so he was able to catch himself and fly back toward me. "Sophia, what's wrong?" Now his voice sounded more forceful this time.

"I gave you everything; I was willing to give up everything for you. But in the end it's not good enough."

"What are you talking about? I love you."

"Do not say you love me," I screamed, and lightning shot out of the sky.

"I don't understand what's going on here."

"Oh act innocent, but did you really think I'm that stupid? I mean honestly, look who you're trying to fool." Now the rain was coming down harder and harder, and the streets were starting to have large puddles everywhere.

"What are you talking about? I'm not trying to fool you. I love you."

"I should kill you, but then you wouldn't feel how I feel right now."

"You need to calm down, look around you. It's getting crazy, and the storm looks out of control."

"Victoria," I shouted.

"What did you say?" Now he had a serious

look. Instead of being worried about me he was looking defensive.

"I met Victoria."

"Victoria who?" He asked, trying to play innocent.

"Your fiancée—or shall I say ex-fiancée." Now I began to walk toward the end of the pier and onto the water.

"What do you mean?"

"Oh, I killed her."

"You did what?" He shouted out.

"Don't worry; I brought the love of your life back from the dead. She's somewhere in this town hiding in some hole."

"Sophia, listen to me," he started to say.

"Listen to what?"

I cut him off because I was too mad to listen. As I took a deep breath lightning struck and then I began to say, "To how you were playing me for a fool, you two-timing dog."

"It's not like that; when you were gone, I searched. But after you kept running away before I could find you, I finally gave up. So I came here to start a life, and that's when I met Victoria. I don't love her, she's just here; so I decided to try and move on. But when I saw you again, I was planning on leaving her." He walked closer to me and said, "I swear."

"You want me to care about anything that comes out of your mouth. If I was the one you love like the way you claim, then you would have waited. No matter how long." The streets were getting flooded in the town; I could feel people beginning to panic.

"You have to trust me; I was going to leave her. I love you and always will." He tried to grab my hand.

"Don't say that ever again. The next time I hear you say that you love me, I will kill you." Now I was pacing back and forth on the water.

"I love you."

"Are you crazy? Have you ever heard of a woman scorned? Now imagine me scorned!"

"You can't kill me. I mean you can, but you won't, because no matter what you still love me." He was right, though, I still loved him; and that's why this hurt all the more.

"Don't tempt me, because if I have to I will. Right now I want you to know that we are through. Any chance of an 'us' is dead."

"Don't do that to yourself."

"To myself? You have some nerve."

"Think of what we could have, the house, the dog, and the baby." Listening to that only made it hurt more. Now that I thought of it, I had all my hopes set high, and I honestly trusted him, only to get burned. Maybe I was evil, because it burned so much right then.

I could hear radio announcements telling everyone to evacuate the town. Every station was the same, warning of this uncontrollable storm. They were calling it Hurricane Katrina; unfortunately, they got the name wrong. I wished I could control my feelings, but I couldn't.

"I don't need you; if I want it, I can have it. You may be immortal, but you're dead to me. Think of me as dead as well, because from this day you will never see me again. I can't believe you think I needed you. I created the damn universe you're living in; if I want something, you're sure as hell not the one to give it to me." I couldn't believe he actually thought that I needed him.

"You don't mean that. You can't give up on love." He grabbed my wrist and pulled me toward him, but this time it hurt. I mean it really hurt; his touch was pain and only pain. Usually when he touched me it was a mixture of pain and pleasure; this time it only hurt.

"Your right, I will give love another chance. Do you remember Lazarus? I think you know him; he's the man who tries to save the souls before you can take them. He's attractive, smart, and he cares about me; he's everything you're not. I wish I would've seen him before I made you, then maybe you would have been created the right way." I would never date Lazarus; I was only saying this to hurt Lucifer. I swore I would make him feel pain, so I would hit him where it hurt.

"Don't you ever say that again!" He grabbed me by my throat and squeezed. He was actually trying to choke me, and it hurt; I'd never felt physical pain before, and this hurt.

"Are you stupid?" I grabbed his hand and crushed it, turning all the bones inside to dust. While his hand was regenerating, I walked behind him, and with one swipe, I ripped off his wings. "I can't believe you dared to put your hands on me. This should teach you to never touch a woman," I said as he fell to his knees screaming. Now I walked away with two big black wings in my hand, watching him crouching on the water.

"Ahhhhhh," he was screaming while on the floor.

His hands were covering his face, and the blood

was pouring down his back. As the blood dripped, it looked like a teabag immersed into water. Slowly the blood mixed with the water, until all around him was red.

"Man up." I said. I dropped the wings, and I watched and they slowly sank into the ocean beneath me.

"You're crazy, this hurts so much," he said as he staggered back onto his feet.

"I thought you were stronger than this." I turned and watched him with my hands folded.

"Why are they not regenerating?" he asked, while biting his teeth down to try and bear the pain. The cuts were starting to heal, but the wings weren't growing back.

"That's because no matter how strong you are, you are no match for me. It's like a rat trying to fight a lion." This poor unfortunate fool thought I was done. The severity of the weather was only intensifying; this fight just began.

"They will never grow back?" he asked. I could see the sadness in his eyes.

The city was getting more and more flooded. But I was not doing this purposely; it was just my emotions coming out of me. Just like what happened the last time, the Earth was reacting to my heart. That's the problem—I built this planet with my heart, and so it gets affected by the way I feel.

"No, I took them off, which means they can never grow back."

"Look around you, look at what you're doing." As I looked around, I could see that the clouds were all black and they were getting lower.

"Do you think I want this to happen? If I could control this storm I would."

"I'm willing to forget this. I still love you and I want you back. Let's just go home and talk about this." I couldn't believe that he still loved me and wanted me back after I took away his flight.

"Go talk to your fiancée, Victoria." I couldn't be so selfish next time. By being so vulnerable, I was putting everyone at risk.

"Sophia, you're so hurt your heart is releasing a hurricane. But this doesn't have to happen. We can still be. Just let it go, and trust me."

"Just let it go and trust you. That's why we're in this mess."

"But I still love you." He touched my hand, and that's the last touch he would ever have.

"I despise you. My love turned to hate. I have no heart anymore. Enjoy your memories, because this is the last time you will ever see me again. I'm much better without you." I looked him in the eye and walked away.

"You're going to be sorry for leaving me."

"I didn't do anything. You did it to yourself."

"You have the power to fix all this. Just look at what you're doing to the city. The hurricane will destroy it."

"The water can wash away my tears."

"Wait."

"No, we're done. Good-bye."

"If you leave I promise you, you'll regret it." I didn't want to leave with the hurricane flooding the streets, but I couldn't stop it. The only chance of this hurricane subsiding is if I left. I had to come to the realization that I was the hurricane.

"Good-bye, forever." When I closed my eye, the winds starting getting so powerful that everything around me was getting destroyed, and before I could do anything, the levees broke. The water went gushing into the town, and as much as it killed me to see what I did, I had to leave. I didn't do it intentionally, but I should never have allowed myself to fall for him. Then this never would have happened. I turned around and continued to walk away from the devastation. The town was flooding, the sky turned black, the winds were gushing, people were dying, and my tears were still falling. So I continued to walk toward the ocean, away from the city; the only hope it had of surviving was if I left now. Each step I took felt harder to make. I closed my eyes and tried to dry them as I walked away.

As I opened my eyes and dried my last tear, the breeze brushed against my cheek, taking my hair up with it. I could feel the hard floor underneath my bare feet. Each step I took, my foot touched the warm rocks, sinking into the cracks. I looked up at the sun and saw a guard in the tower. He smiled at me, but I had no more smiles to give. I continued to take one step after another, on the longest trail in the world. Down this Great Wall I walk alone, each step as lonely as the one before.

Breinigsville, PA USA
16 November 2010

249441BV00001B/9/P